Starkey's Gold

I'd waited a long time for the man to walk in to my bar and confront me. Now it was over and he lay on the ground very dead as I held a smoking shotgun in my hand. I knew my secret was safe. But how wrong can a man be?

It was only the beginning of a new kind of hell. Another ghost from my past came to visit me – a man whom I'd been responsible for sending to jail. He was determined to know the secret I had kept hidden for thirty years.

But to wrest that secret from me would endanger my daughter Amy, and so I knew I faced a fight to the death.

Starkey's Gold

NEWTON KETTON

A Black Horse Western

ROBERT HALE · LONDON

Typeset by
Derek Doyle & Associates, Liverpool
Printed and bound in Great Britain by
Antony Rowe Limited, Wiltshire

ONE

I looked across the bar to the man sprawled on the floor and then at the smoking shotgun in my hand. I drew a deep breath. It was over. The long years of waiting and wondering when he would catch up with me, were over. It was finished. My secret was safe.

For a moment I was stunned, then reaction set in. I wanted to prance and yell like an Apache counting coup, but my old legs wouldn't let me. Instead I reached for the bottle and poured myself a generous measure of rotgut whiskey.

Then the batwing doors swung open and I turned around with the whiskey glass in one hand and the other too damn far away from the shotgun on the bartop to do any good.

I stared into the mocking eyes of Ike Jordache. The last time I'd seen him he was but a stripling. Now he was a hard-faced mountain of a man with cold-as-death blue eyes and a grizzled beard.

'It's been a long time, Starkey!'

I licked my lips, then slid my eyes over the man on the floor. Jordache's eyes followed mine. He looked ruminatively at him, scratching his beard.

'So, Bill got here before me!' There was no emotion or chagrin. He spoke matter of factly, as if the killing was unimportant. Then he smiled and fear rippled up and down my spine. 'So there's only you and me now, Starkey.'

He motioned to the inner room behind the bar and quietly swung his duster coat free of his gunbelt. I stared in fascination. He still carried the pearl-handled Peacemakers I'd had specially made all those long years ago. His hands hovered over the gun butts. His heavy lips puckered.

'Would be ironic if your guns ended your miserable life!'

My knees shook and my legs felt like jelly. It's a helluva sensation to look down two gun barrels, especially when they once belonged to a feller.

'We must talk,' I croaked, holding my hands high so that he didn't get any wrong messages. My mind had been spinning with shock but now I was calming down. The old iron nerve was coming back. If you've got it, it never really leaves you, no matter how old you are.

I never expected to reach fifty, never mind sixty. I was old enough to die anyway. I had nothing to lose, now that I'd got over the shock of seeing him again.

I knew he wouldn't kill me, maybe plug a hole or two in me but nothing vital. Not until he knew my secret. After that, who knows?

Why, do you ask?

Because he and I are the last of the gang who robbed the gold bullion-train guarded by the military on its way to the Treasury in Washington. It was a military campaign all right. Ike Jordache had been a major with a grudge and he knew how to plot a campaign. He had the brains and I had the men with the muscle.

I was the one who masterminded where to cache the stuff and I made sure the location was kept secret. But plans don't always work out as they should. I shot all the men involved but one man got away. He was now dead on the floor in my saloon.

I never thought to see Ike Jordache again. A little forethought on my part had seen that an anonymous tip-off had led to Jordache being banged up in the penitentiary for twenty-five years.

I calculated that he must have been out for the last six years.

'What took you so long in finding me?' I asked surlily.

He shrugged. 'It's a big world out there. I got on to Bill's trail and all I had to do was follow him and let him do the work. Now we'll talk. 'He motioned me into the inner room.

I looked around helplessly. There was only the town drunk in the saloon, and he was in cloud-cuckoo-land. It was a quiet period. All my buddies were off on the big round-up of cattle for the branding.

I walked before him; he followed and kicked the door shut with a scuffed boot. I turned and stared at him. I saw the hatred in his eyes. They glowed red.

'Now, if you sit in that chair and put your hands behind you, I'll make you comfortable and we can talk. If not, I'll blast both your kneecaps. Right?'

I nodded.

I knew when to do as I was told.

I cursed my carelessness as he bound my wrists tight.

I wondered how long I could last before I was forced to tell him what he wanted to know and in what condition I would be to at the end of it.

It was all in the lap of the gods.

TWO

My chin touched my chest, my eyes were too heavy to open. There was a buzzing in my ears and I tasted blood on my lips. I was conscious of tight ropes biting into my upper arms and chest, while my hands, bound behind my back, screamed their agony as they swelled, blood-engorged.

A faint voice wavering in the air said persuasively, 'William? Be a good boy and answer the questions.'

I stirred. Only my mother, God bless her, ever called me William. What was she doing here? She'd been dead for years. I raised my head with an effort and could have sworn I saw her flickering shadow. Then the icy cold water hit me in the face and Ma was gone for ever.

I gasped and spluttered like a spitted trout. Another slosh of water hit me and I opened my eyes with a curse and saw Ike Jordache grinning at me, his yellow teeth reminding me of a wolf I killed back in '57.

'Blast you, Jordache! You interrupted a dream,' I muttered.

His answer was a backhanded slap across my mouth.

'Never mind dreamin', old man. Where's that gold?'

I've always been a fool. I laughed in his face. I was a burning-up wreck, with every nerve in my rotten body screaming for release. But I wouldn't give him the satisfaction of tearing that secret from me.

'It's all in m' head, buster,' I slurred mockingly. He hit me again. I was past caring. I couldn't hurt any more than I was at this moment.

I watched him walk up and down my small back room which I used as an office. It was sparsely furnished: a battered desk, three chairs, a cupboard for holdin' liquor and a few shelves holdin' mementoes of my long life. On the wall above the open fireplace was a badly painted picture of my wife.

He raided my cupboard and found a bottle of

whiskey. He opened it and gulped thirstily, my own gullet heaving in time with his. I could have done with a snort.

He looked at the painting and turned suddenly to me.

'Do you realize what you did to me, Starkey, when you got me banged up? I was twenty-five years old and you robbed me of havin' what you had,' pointing to the picture. 'I never saw or smelt a woman in all those years when I was breaking rocks, except in m' dreams. D'you know what it's like to bed a woman and wake up to find all you've got is a wet bed and no woman?'

My first reaction was to grin but then suddenly my heart froze. I had a daughter....

I think he saw my face change. He leaned forward and poked me in the chest.

'Why don't you answer me? Have you ever had a wet dream, Starkey, or are you one of the lucky ones who always had a bedmate? What about her?' He poked a thumb in the direction of the picture.

'She's dead.'

'But there must have been others?'

'Yeah, I've had my share.'

'Good. So now you won't mind your balls bein' shot off?'

I stirred uneasily. The thought gave me a new pain. If I was to be shot, it wouldn't be deliberate. I didn't want to live as a geldin'. I drew up my legs and the chair went backwards. I caught him as he bent over me, right in the bollocks. That would show him.

I expected him to rise and blast me in the chest, but he didn't. He rolled and squawked like some cockerel bein' neutered. A big man but a little 'un when it came to endurin' pain. Army majors were always soft. It was the common soldier who took on the enemy and in the case of soldiers unlucky enough to be prisoners of the Apache or the Sioux, if they lived, it was because they could withstand torture.

I'd been one of those men. I'd been slow-burned over a fire and had the scars to prove it.

Now I watched, with detached amusement, this fat bloated bastard rollin' about the floor like a screamin' infant. I spat in contempt.

But his screamin' saved me. The door was flung open and Luke Channing burst in, his gun waving like a mad thing.

'Jesus, Starkey, what's goin' on?' He was starin' at me all bound up and then at Jordache rollin' about on the floor.

'Knock the bastard out,' I snapped, 'and stop

gawpin' and cut me loose.'

Luke's crack on the head put Jordache out cold, and soon I was free. I was mighty shaken but I wasn't lettin' Luke Channing know that. He was an arrogant young pup as it was. I had to keep a thumb on him because he was sparkin' Amy and he was the best young sheriff Apache Springs had ever had. He kept the town drunks in order and confiscated firearms from all strangers comin' into town.

He was the reason the secret of the gold remained a secret. I was now respectable, having used some of that bullion raid to buy me a good saloon as well as a good-sized ranch. I'd fought hard to be respectable and give my daughter a good life.

No bastard like Ike Jordache was goin' to come after all these years and mess things up.

Like it or not, Jordache was destined to be dropped in a crevice of rock out there in the wilderness. I couldn't allow him to live.

The decision didn't worry me. All I was worried about was Amy and Luke finding out about my shady past. I couldn't allow that. Ike Jordache had to die.

*

Luke was for putting Jordache in jail, chargin' him with assault, attempt to murder with robbery in mind and anything else he could think of. He was amazed and indignant when I said no. I was goin' to ride him out of town, give him a thrashin' and send him on his way hogtied to his hoss. That would teach him not to come back to Apache Springs.

Luke thought I was mad and so did Amy, who dissolved into floods of tears, remindin' me I wasn't as young as I used to be and that Jordache would somehow kill me.

I pointed out that Jordache's wrists would be bound behind him, so how the hell could he kill me?

Luke fish-eyed me in a very funny way. He knew I was up to somethin'. I couldn't very well tell him I was goin' to backshoot the bastard and drop him in a gully. I only wanted to be away and do the business.

I ached in every limb and my jaw stung and the few teeth I had seemed looser than they should be. The pain kept my anger burnin'. Ike Jordache's passin' wouldn't be easy....

In spite of protests I had my way. We moved out, he with his wrists bound tight and rigged to the pommel of his saddle and me bristlin' with firearms. I was takin' no chances.

We left town by the back trail and rode into the foothills. I knew the very place to do for the bastard: Lookout Pass, a high lonely place with deep crevices and a long gorge with the river flowin' through it, lookin' like a snail's trail far below.

It was a wild and windy place and only fools or desperate men on the look-out for trouble would linger there. It was a fittin' place for Jordache to haunt, if one believed in an after-life.

The horses picked their way carefully, both were experienced mountain nags and there was no words between us. His head was low on his chest. Mebbe I'd hurt him more than I expected. I was busy thinkin' about the hidin' I was goin' to give him before shootin' him. We went back a long way and there was things in the past I wanted to make him pay for, such as the killin' of my best buddy, Larry and his whuppin' of me at the time when he took my Peacemakers from me . .. the weals on my back still itched when I sweated and had always reminded me of him. The hate was and always had been there....

I looked down at those Peacemakers. One of

them would blow the bastard to hell, which was only fittin'.

My horse stumbled. I cursed. We had nearly come to the pass and the sun was high but the sharp breeze kept us moderately cool. He looked at me for the first time on that journey and gave a crooked smile.

'You sound uptight, Starkey. Your nerves are twangin' like harp strings. You're past it, Starkey. What about doin' a deal?'

'You're in no position for makin' deals, mister,' I growled, ignorin' the needlin' about my age.

'I could let you in on a government secret.'

I pricked up my ears. 'You've got no secret. You're havin' me on.'

He laughed and shrugged. 'Am I? It's to do with the new railroad comin' in these parts.'

That made a difference. A railroad would mean no more trailin' herds to Abilene. A rancher in the know could arrange for a spur line to load up his cows. It would make a mighty difference if the cows didn't walk their meat off before they got to the stockyards and the time difference would be stupendous.

My mind boggled.

'Look, I've got belly cramps. I'll have to shit,'

he said while I was considerin' his words. 'Why not stop and rest the hosses and we can talk about this and I can have a shit.'

I scratched my head and rubbed a raspy chin. I hadn't reckoned on stoppin'. I'd planned on draggin' him off his horse and givin' him a whuppin' like he give me and then shootin' him before droppin' him down into a deep hole. All finished.

He was lookin' rough. I didn't care about him havin' the shits but I sure would have liked to hear about this railroad business.

I could always listen to him and then do the job, I reasoned. No sweat. I didn't believe in deals or promises. Both were made to be broken. In fact, he could do me a good turn which would make him turn over and over in whatever grave he fell in.

Reluctantly I cut his wrist bonds. He rubbed his hands together to bring back the circulation and I was a fool, I stood and watched and suddenly I got a foot jabbed right in my bollocks. As I rolled away in agony I got a glimpse of him laughing like a maniac as his other leg came over the horse and he sprang down beside me, his foul breath in my face.

'You didn't think it would be that easy to

bring me up into these here hills and blast me, did you? I'm surprised at you, Starkey, fallin' for the railroad gag.'

'So it wasn't true?'

'Oh, it's true enough. At least it's been talked about in Washington. I have ears there, y'know. But now we're talkin' about that gold.'

I spat up at his face and a gob hit him on the cheek. He didn't blink. He was used to slime. He was made of it.

'You can go to hell!' I snarled. He slapped me and I tasted blood. Then he gave me a rabbit-punch and I passed out.

I was lyin' aboard my horse, my head hangin' low so I could see the ground below. The joggin' of the beast was agony. My balls were on fire. Alongside me, Jordache rode easily, holdin' my horse's rein.

'Where are we headin'?' I croaked.

'To your ranch, Starkey. I want to meet your daughter. They say she's a mighty purty girl.'

'What d'you want with her?' As if I didn't know!

He looked my way and grinned, a purely evil grin.

'I never pass up a chance of a woman, Starkey. I've a lot of makin' up to do because of you, and the way I figure it is, that what I can't beat outta you, I can get it easy by barterin' her young virginity against the whereabouts of that there bullion. Savvy? Figure it out for yourself.'

I set my teeth. The agony in my guts was nothin' to the agony in my mind about my girl. I thought of her. She would go back to the ranch after we left and wait for me. There would only be old Russ, my manager, and Anita, the house-keeper, and the two old Mexicans who did the chores about the place while the younger cowhands went about their business out on the range.

There would be no contest against a man like Jordache who would take them by surprise. They would all be catsmeat.

'If I tell you what you want to know is there a deal?'

'A deal? Like you pointed out, Starkey, you're not in a position to deal.'

I shut my trap. I'd have to think of something else.

I wondered if Luke would accompany Amy back to the ranch. He was my only hope. Luke could help load the dice my way. He was a shoo-tist and took pride in the speed of his reactions.

His draw was second to none.

Jordache might yet get a surprise.

The sun was going down when we came in sight of the ranch. We'd passed under the arch which showed the Circle S brand which was burned on all Starkey cows and horses. I could never look over that range and not relive all the hassle and danger and hard work I'd gone through in the past to get where I was today.

But now I had no thought of myself. My mind was filled with Amy and her ma, who'd died ten years ago in childbirth when Amy was eight years old. There had been no other woman in our house except for Anita since that time. My world was Amy. Everything was for her. Now my baby was in danger. I knew that even if I spilled my guts and told him everything, he wouldn't spare Amy. He was not that kind of man. One look at her perty face and buddin' figure and the animal in him would take over....

Me, I wasn't no prayin' man but I sure as hell prayed to anyone up there willin' to listen to a sinner like me, to help my girl. It didn't matter about me. I'd done a whole heap of sinnin' in my time and reckoned I was past redemption anyway. But my Amy was too young to have lived or sinned. She had a right to her life and I argued this out with God, if there was such a one.

My mind was babblin' as he cut me loose and I fell heavily to the ground. I rolled and groaned in agony. It was real, that agony, but not as bad as I made out. If he'd come too close I should have grabbed his ankle and brought him down and then it would have been a fight to the death.

But the bastard was too cute. He hollered the house.

'Ho there the house! Anyone home?'

For a few fleetin' moments I thought that Amy had not yet returned, but just as my heart leapt joyously in my chest, she opened the screen door and I heard her voice and her running feet.

'I'm sorry. If you want my father, he's away from home.' Then I heard the quaver come into her voice as she asked, 'Who's that on the ground? Is he hurt?' Then she was bendin' over me, her cool hands on my chin as she turned my head to look at me. She gasped. 'Pa, are you all right?' Her flutterin' hands were all over me, seekin' a wound.

23

Then that rotten slime-eatin' bastard was pullin' her from me and she screamed and fought as I scrabbled to get to my feet. A bullet splattered the ground inches from my head, dust flyin', almost blindin' me.

'Don't move, Starkey. I could just as easily put a slug in your knee, but I want you in one piece to take me to that gold. Now do you play straight with me or would you like to watch me play games with this little filly? She's a fair armful and I sure am itchy.'

'Harm her, Jordache and you'll live to regret it.' I wasn't spoutin' off out of bravado. I had seen a movement behind Jordache. The report of the gun had brought someone runnin'.

Ike Jordache laughed at me. 'Tough words, Starkey but they don't mean shit! I'm gettin' just a little impatient. If you don't begin to talk by the time I count three, I'll start strippin' her.'

I saw Amy begin to shake and Jordache was havin' a job holdin' her upright. Her face was as pale as white linen and her terror cut right into my heart. I was filled with such rage that I was nearly blinded by a red haze.

My hand grasped a fistful of dust and I threw it in their faces. Amy screamed and Jordache swore and as I rolled away, a gun blasted, followed by another report. Jordache swung Amy away and, turning, shot at the tell-tale puff of smoke from the first gun.

I heard the body fall and thought Jordache still had the luck of the devil. I clawed my way upwards but Jordache was already draggin' Amy away to his horse.

Before I could get to him, he'd flung her aboard and was preparin' to leap astride and thunder out of the yard.

'If you want her back, Starkey, meet me in Apache Pass. I'll give you until midnight. After that, the girl is mine and you'll never see her again!' With that, they rode away and I was left with stumblin' legs that felt like jelly, a head fit to bust and a crotch so tender I could have cried like a baby.

I forced myself to go back to the body, which was lying still. I felt sick. I imagined Luke Channing lying there, but when I turned the body over it was Russ, my good loyal old buddy. I didn't know whether to be glad or sorry. I wanted Luke alive for Amy's sake, but I would miss Russ every day for the rest of my miserable life.

I saw Anita watchin' fearfully from behind the kitchen door. I cursed her and told her to stop gawpin' and find the peons. It had to be a quick burial in all this heat. I must have sounded cold and unfeelin' for she gave me a strange look and scurried away. I was grievin' inside but I couldn't show it. My mind was on Amy and how to get her back.

I needed a plan and my head was too jumbled to think straight. I needed a drink badly. Mebbe a couple of stiff drinks would get the old brain cells workin'.

I was pourin' a third drink when the plan took shape. I must get back to Luke as quick as possible. I faced the fact that, capable as I was, it had been years since I'd mounted up a heist of any kind. I needed help from a man I could trust and who better than Luke, who loved Amy?

I should get an earful for bein' a stubborn old fool in the first place. I should never have ridden off with Jordache as I had done. I was just a dodderin' old fool in Luke's eyes. He didn't know about my past. Nevertheless, the boy would go along with what we had to do now.

Reluctantly I concluded that at long last I must tell him the secret of the gold. As he was a smart boy who could add up and come up with right answers, I was goin' to have to concoct a story about how half a million dollars in gold bars was in a location only I knew of.

It was goin' to take some mighty fancy talkin' to come up with a reasonable explanation.

THREE

I was right. Luke cursed me to hell and back when I finally gasped out what had happened. He still hadn't figured anythin' beyond the fact that Amy was took off by Jordache. I had never seen him in such a rage, not even when the town drunk got hold of Amy one Thanksgivin' and kissed her on the lips.

'Cre-ist! You half-witted old fool! We told you … begged you, but would you listen? Now what do we do?' He sounded like a hen that had lost her chicks.

'Shaddup and listen!' I slapped his face, for I thought he was gonna have a fit or somethin'. His eyes bulged and he fingered his cheek but it did the trick. He stopped squawkin' and glared at me.

'Well? What are we goin' t'do?'

'We've got 'til midnight. We're gonna ride out there as if all hell was after us, and we're gonna take the son of a bitch by surprise.'

'Just the two of us? I could raise a posse.'

'No. Two of us can do it. There's no sayin' what he would do to Amy if he saw a posse comin' after him. Have you still got that dynamite left over from clearin' out the Schneider gang in Battle Gorge?'

'Yeah, a dozen sticks or so. They shoulda gone back to headquarters but the marshal forgot about 'em.'

'Good. We'll tote 'em with us. They could be mighty useful.'

Luke looked at me as if he'd never seen me before. 'Can you handle dynamite? It's tricky stuff.'

I laughed. If only he knew! I'd used more explosives than he'd had suck from his ma. He didn't know the real me and I didn't want him to, but if it meant him knowin' and savin' Amy, well then what would be would be....

'Son, I was clearin' trees before you were born and blastin' boulders as big as houses when I was just a fledglin'. My pa said I had a real talent for it. He called me Smokey Bill.' It was

30

a lie but I had to come up with somethin'. He nodded. He could take that, for he and his pa had worked well together until his pa up and died.

'I'll go get it and we'll take extra guns and ammo and some grub.'

I smiled. Now the kid's brains were workin'.

We nearly killed our horses. It was all uphill work when we got into the foothills. When twilight fell it was hard goin' as the horses stumbled and panted until we had to dismount for the racket they made.

We shouldered the packs after tetherin' the horses and havin' a cold meal. I could have used a gallon of coffee but we stuck with water as a fire would show up for miles.

Then it was one hard slog to the summit of Apache Pass. The moon was just beginnin' to show and we crouched on the skyline lookin' down into the pass itself. There was no movement or sign of life. I cursed under my breath. Had the bastard decided on a new tactic?

I knew he would be around somewhere. He wanted me more than he wanted Amy. Or maybe he'd already used Amy ... I daren't think of that possibility. I glanced at Luke's white face and knew he was thinkin' the same as me.

I put a hand on his arm.

'Don't even think it! Keep calm. We'll get the bastard, never fear,' I growled in an undertone. 'Just wait!'

Luke was impatient. He was young, his mind more on Amy than on the situation in hand. I was tryin' to keep cool and not think too much about my girl. All I wanted was to locate the bastard.

'What about throwin' a stick of dynamite down there, and scarin' the daylights out of him,' breathed Luke in my ear.

'And lose our advantage of surprise? D'you want to panic him into killin' Amy, you blasted fool!' I answered viciously. 'Just hold your hosses, Luke, and keep your damned mouth shut!' All the time my eyes were stabbin' the darkness for the least sign of movement.

Then I thought I saw a shadow move. It could have been a coyote on the prowl but instinct took over; I gripped Luke's shoulder and nodded towards it. Luke was for racin' forward and doin' somethin' stupid. I pulled him back.

'Wait here,' I whispered in his ear, 'and don't make a move until I whistle for you. Now remember, no rushin' in or he might shoot her. Get it?'

He nodded and I bellied my way towards the

shadow that was no shadow. I was exultant. I was sure I'd come up behind the bastard and could take him before he had time to spit. He was goin' to get a hell of a surprise.

But it was me who got the surprise. I stuck my gun in the back of Jordache and said softly,

'All right, Jordache, where is she?'

He turned and it was then I saw he wasn't Jordache but some lowdown scum who smelt of badly cured skins. He turned like an animal, showed his teeth and struck out at me. I pulled myself together and let him have it, cursin' as the report of the gun sent birds flappin' in their roosts and nocturnal hunters scurried away.

I heard a great brayin' of laughter, like some hyena findin' a cache of dead meat and I was the meat. Then Ike Jordache was lookin' down at me, gun pointin' at my belly and him so pleased with himself he was like a kid at a Sunday-School treat.

I was aware of somethin' else too. I was surrounded by the best bunch of cut-throats I'd seen in years.

I could only stare up at him. I sure was hornswoggled. I hadn't thought of him havin' a gang with him. I'd reckoned he was just a lone wolf. Now I knew different.

He squatted down and peered in my face.

'You think you could outsmart me, Starkey? I'm not just some hunk of shit. I've got brains between my ears, mister. Now, are you goin' to talk or do I persuade you by amusin' myself with that gal of yours?'

I didn't answer. I was thinking swiftly and only hoped Luke wouldn't come crashing down and joinin' in the fun. Jordache kicked me. I felt a rib crack. I groaned.

Another kick made me squirm away from him and a little skinny feller who later I found answered to Danny twisted a rope about my wrists.

'Should I string him up, boss?'

I struggled like a cat caught in a trap but it was no good. My rib let me down. I cursed myself for bein' too clever and for the first time wondered whether I really was too old to be smart any more.

'What about it, Starkey? Do I have fun with your gal or will you talk?'

'How do I know she's still with you?'

'Oh, she's here all right. Danny, go bring her here and let Starkey see she's still in one piece. Mebbe she can knock some sense into you. After all, I'm entitled to know what you know,

Starkey. We were all in the heist together. I only want what's mine.'

'You didn't run the risk we did. You ran with the hare and hunted with the hounds.'

'I gave you the information!'

'But you stayed with the army as one of the officers huntin' us! You were a double traitor, to the army and to us, Jordache. D'your men think you'll play fair and square with them when you get your hands on that gold? No sir! You'll do the dirty like you did with us.'

'And who the hell are you to talk, Starkey? You were as bad! There was only Bill Whylam got away from you. I got all the details from him. You two-timed your own gang, Starkey.'

'There were reasons,' I growled. 'They were in your pay, Jordache, and I overheard the bastards talkin' about the big pay-outs when you joined them after they'd shot me up. I wasn't havin' that, so I killed the lot of 'em. It was a pity Bill got away when he did.'

He glared down at me. I was ready to make a last stand when there was an interruption and Danny was draggin' Amy over to us.

I must say, Amy had spunk. It took all the little feller's strength to drag her along. Then she saw me and screamed.

'Pa! Are you all right?' She slapped Danny on the jaw, flung herself down beside me and hugged me and damn me, if she didn't kiss me, somethin' she hadn't done since she was a kid. I can't describe the feelin' I had. Joy and confusion mainly but enough to ignore the kick Jordache swiped at me, narrowly missin' my busted rib.

I rolled and groaned, a great red rage reachin' up from my feet to the top of m'head. It gave me the strength to scramble to my feet as I lashed out at the evil bastard. I caught him a hearty wallop in the balls before Danny and a couple more scumbags overpowered me again and I took a leatherin' that made me gasp.

They hung on to me while Jordache grabbed Amy despite his sore crotch. At least rapin' my girl would be the last thing on his mind.

I wondered what had become of Luke. I hoped to God he wouldn't try to play the hero and come out shootin' to grab Amy. He would have no chance. Patience was what was needed now and I hoped to God he had the sense to know that.

'Well, now, mebbe we should use other tactics,' Jordache said softly. I'd heard that tone before long years ago. Jordache was at his most dangerous when he spoke in that soft cultured accent. I'd often wondered about his background in the past, bein' an army officer an' all. I think he come from good stock and that was why when scandal broke out and he was cut adrift from the army life he knew, his pride couldn't take it. That was what made him the vicious maniac he was today.

Danny whispered in his ear and they moved away. I could read Danny's ferretty face and knew he'd thought up something special for me. I promised myself that if I got free, I'd cut off his genitals and stuff 'em down his rat-trap throat. I'd make him chew 'em good and watch him swallow 'em and then I'd rip his guts open and drag 'em out and show 'em to him as he died.'

Jordache laughed and barked an order to his two scumbags.

'Tie him to that dead tree yonder, boys. We'll have us a roastin'. The little lady here won't let her good father die like a trussed up turkey. She'll do whatever you boys want to keep him alive! Tonight, you're all goin' to have a treat, boys! How d'you feel about that?'

There was cheerin' and catcalls and my heart sank. I wasn't havin' that. Better to give the slimeball what he wanted. What the hell ... gettin' at the gold bullion would be no Sunday-School tea-party even when he knew where it was stashed.

'Hold it, Jordache! I'll tell you what you want to know but not if those thugs of yours get all-fired up with thoughts of usin' my girl to slake their lust.'

'Mebbe it's gone too far, Starkey. You played mum too long.'

'Look, if you tell 'em that their share of the bullion could buy them a whole heap of women more experienced than a young girl who doesn't know it's more than just to piss out of!'

Jordache had a faraway look in his eyes.

'You mean what you say? You'll tell me?'

'Yes, I'll tell you, providin' you keep those hogs of yours off her.'

His eyes narrowed.

'You and the girl are comin' with us, Starkey. I don't trust you and if you lie to me, I'll skin you alive!'

'I'll not lie. I want Amy alive and untouched after this is over.'

'You're very confident, Starkey. What if I can't hold my boys off her?'

'Then you can kiss the gold goodbye.'

His eyes sparked dangerously. 'We've got to trust each other!'

'Yeah, two old mountain goats cuttin' and thrustin'. I'll trust you just as much as you'll trust me!'

'Then what do we do?'

'For a start, you can cut me loose and Amy too. We're not goin' anywhere, you've too many men for us to do that and I sure won't go anywhere without her.'

'And?'

'I'll guide you to the treasure but you won't get the true location until we get there. I'm not riskin' tellin' you everything and gettin' my throat cut afterwards.'

'Hmm, fair enough. I can't see you getting away from us. We're too many for you and the girl would hold you back. Yes, I can go along with those arrangements. Mind you, there'll be guards watching you twenty-four hours a day.'

'Yeah, that figures. Still, the officer givin' out orders. Now what about givin' us some grub? I can figure out the route better if I'm a well-fed man.'

I stretched and straightened my achin' back to judge the condition of my hurt rib. I reckoned it was a crack. I'd had one years ago and it mended in a matter of days, but I sure wasn't lettin' on to Jordache.

'I got a rib bust and I want Amy to bind it up for me. I suppose you'll let a daughter minister to her old man?'

He shoved Amy towards me. 'Use his bandanna, honey, and make it quick.'

While my guards watched from a distance with guns at the ready, he walked away to the camp-fire to see about grub. I managed a quick whisper in Amy's ear.

'Courage, lass. I'll get us outta this. Just go along with 'em and stick close. I got 'em figured.'

She shivered and looked at me doubtfully, her fingers trembling as she fashioned a crude bandage for my rib. I knew what she was thinkin'. Her old man was past it. She'd never known my wild side. That had been long ago and I wasn't very happy about lettin' her see me as I really was. Still, if everything went as I planned, mebbe I could figure an excuse for why I suddenly got a rush of blood to the head. After all, a feller is entitled to protect his young. That was the least of my worries.

I knew there was no way I could tell her about Luke. Amy was an honest straightfor-ward kid and her expression would alert

40

Jordache that somethin' was up if she knew that Luke was close by.

No, I had to have patience, go along with what Jordache wanted and watch out for that opportunity which would surely come. I'd experienced danger in the past and could always guarantee that at some time the enemy's vigilance would slip. Mind you, this was some situation because of Jordache's men. He was takin' no chances with me. That was my bad luck, him knowin' how I could react.

I settled myself against a tree when Amy was done. She sat close to me, head down, and I prepared to play the wounded soldier. No need to let Jordache know that my rib was mebbe only bruised. I had more go in me than he realized.

One of his men brought two steamin' plates of stew. I took mine willin'ly. You had to eat to keep up strength. I glanced at Amy who only stared at her own steamin' plate.

'Eat,' I barked and she was surprised at my tone. Her eyes filled as she looked at me and I felt like a monster. But I kept up the bullyin' tone. 'Eat, m'girl! Stuff it down even if you want to be sick! You've gotta keep up your strength. You clean that there plate up or I'll hot up your arse!'

Tears flowed but I was pleased to see she dug in her spoon and began to eat.

Later, when the moon was up and Amy had cried herself to sleep beside me, Jordache came and squatted down real close. He looked at Amy's sleepin' form.

'I'm keepin' my promise, Starkey. The boys won't touch her as long as you go along with us and play no tricks. We ride before dawn. How's the ribs?'

I moved clumsily and groaned.

'Bad, but I'll survive, I reckon.'

He rubbed his chin and then, before I knew what he was about, he thumped me in the chest. I yelled. It really did hurt and I wasn't actin'.

'You bastard!' I yelped hoarsely because I was winded too. 'What you do that for?'

'Just to make sure you weren't playin' silly beggars. You're up to all kinds of tricks, Starkey. I'll be watchin' you constant, never fear.' With that he rose up smoothly from his hunkers and walked away. I cursed him under my breath.

The sun was barely up when we moved out. We had a long way to go and Jordache was takin' no chances. I was trussed like a chicken on my horse and Amy rode alongside me. At least her bonds were not too tight. I'll give the feller his due, he was treatin' her good, and I was not goin' to do anythin' to change his mind.

'You OK, honey?' I asked her. She gave me a tremulous smile and nodded, and I knew she had a little bit of me in her, despite her takin' after her ma. She had spunk, that kid.

We had a lot of travellin' to do, and Jordache knew just how far we'd travelled west after the raid. He'd got all the details from Bill except for the vital location of the bullion itself.

I'd been cute. The boys had stashed it in a gully and covered it with stones. After I heard what was supposed to happen to me I killed the bastards in a blind rage, but Bill had got away. I'd manhandled every goddam chest of gold bars myself and hid them where God himself couldn't find them. I reckoned that if there was one man left, that gold would never be safe and so I sweated and cursed as I moved the lot. Now I thanked God I had done so. Bill had evidently gone back to the stash and found nothin' but an empty gully and a mishmash of stones that had covered it. Serve the swine right!

I remembered the long hard trail as I'd ridden at a gruellin' pace west to outdistance any pursuit. I'd reckoned on at least a couple of days' start before the bullion was missed, and I'd been right.

Now as I rode I was busy thinkin' about the bullion's location and how I could fox Jordache. It was not goin' to be an easy job.

I kept my eye out for any signs of Luke. Up until now he'd been playin' it smart, I wondered how he would make contact. Still, he had brains. He was no meathead. I was relyin' on him more than I'd ever relied on anyone before.

We made our way back east by north to the Carracas foothills where the great canyon cut across country and the swift Ocero River swept through it, cutting its way like a knife. It was lonely, wild country, given over to sand and scrub and stands of stunted pines. The wind blew hard and only fools and criminals would hang out there.

Jordache knew what kind of country it was and loaded up on water and grub. It was goin' to be a long haul.

FOUR

It sure was a long haul and one I'll never forget as long as I live. It wasn't because of my sufferin', it was because of Amy. It was my fault, my stubbornness, that was putting her at that monster's mercy, and no father should have to face that. I think I was loco at that time. Visions of choking the bastard haunted me.

Luke told me afterwards how he followed us usin' Indian tactics. He said little about his fear for Amy and his anger against Jordache. But the very fact that he couldn't talk about it said it all. He'd been a tormented young feller. Durin' the day he rode a coupla hours behind us. At night he left his campsite and stole in and looked us all over. But never once did I suspect. I was beginnin' to despair that Luke had let Amy and me down. But one night he'd managed to have a swift word with Amy when she'd gone into the bushes to relieve herself.

I knew by her face somethin' had happened. Luke had wanted to spirit her away but she wouldn't go account of me, so he gave her a message for me. If there was a chance of gettin' away I was to hoot like a night owl after dark and he would be around with all guns blazin' and a bundle of sticks of dynamite to cause a diversion.

I felt better when I knew the boy hadn't vamoosed. I felt shame that I had come to doubt him. So I gave Amy a lecture on hidin' her feelin's and remindin' her that Jordache was like a prowlin' jaguar with eyes like a hawk's and he'd be watchin' right smart if she grew more cheerful.

I must say she took my words to heart and after that rode with her head down and shoulders slumped like she had lost all hope. I was proud of her.

Meanwhile we journeyed onwards and I began to recognize the terrain. I knew we weren't far off the Carracas foothills with the far mountains lookin' a hazy blue-grey beyond. Soon we should hit the Ocero River that tumbled swiftly through the mighty gorge and it would be then that I'd have to keep my brains sharp if I wanted to best this son of a bitch and his stinkin' scumbags.

I sighed, thinking back to that time. I rubbed my forehead and took a drink from the stone jar at my feet. My throat was dry. I remembered the moment when all hell let loose.

We had just spied the river as it entered the great gorge. It gurgled and roared as it plunged through the narrow gap in the cliffs, white spume risin' so's it looked misty and everythin' was wet. All around was lush greenery which rested the eyes after days of ridin' over parched sun-scorched earth.

There was a chatterin' of birds in the trees which set Jordache off blastin' away as if he thought Indians or devils were all around us.

The rest of the men were jumpy too, as we made our way through the jungle-like growth. But the drippin' water from the leaves was refreshin' after such a dry ride.

Of course we were not travellin' exactly the same route we'd followed before, for then we had two covered wagons carryin' the bullion. Jordache kept watchin' me, seemin' uneasy, as if he suspicioned I was makin' a monkey outta him.

At last he came alongside me and pulled out his gun.

'Are we on the right track, Starkey? If you're holdin' out on me I'll make sure you never walk again!'

I glared at him.

'Would I risk foolin' you with Amy here? Use your head, Jordache. We were bringin' in two wagons. We came the long ways round. Now we're takin' a short cut.'

He gave me a long level look and then nodded.

'Right. Just remember I'm watchin' you at all times, Starkey. I know what a slippery fish you was.'

Amy gave me a puzzled glance and then looked away. I'd always been a quiet respectable father to the lass. Now she couldn't believe all the hints and innuendoes she'd heard. I expect it was like hearin' about a complete stranger.

An hour later, we rounded a great towerin' finger of granite which I recognized and I knew we were at the location. I drew in a long breath.

Now the fun would start.

I pulled my horse to a standstill and pointed.

'There y'are, Jordache. It's all yours … if you can get it!'

He looked blank, the men crowdin' behind him looked bewildered too. I wanted to grin but I controlled myself except for a sudden twitch of the lips.

I noticed that the scene down below seemed to have changed a little over the years. There was a fall of rock for one thing and where the meagre soil was exposed seedlin's were growin' now. It figured in that wet atmosphere. But I was confident. The cave in which I'd hidden the bullion was there all right.

Suddenly Jordache lashed out at me and if I'd caught the full whack I'd have been flung clean out of the saddle. But my horse saw the lunge and stepped aside, still, I felt the draught as his fist came at me. I reacted automatically and grabbed his wrist; with a yank he was on the ground. Then I heard the clickin' of several weapons bein' cocked and I saw that one wrong move and I could be blasted. It was what I knew and they didn't that saved me.

Jordache scrambled to his feet, face red. He was furious.

'You son of a bitch, you're tryin' to fool me with your devilry! I can't see no cache!'

'No, you won't, mister. It's down there along by the river. I can lead you to it, but I can't give you instructions for you'd never find it!'

He took in several, angry breaths. 'If you're stallin', Starkey,' he began.

'Now why should I do that? What good would it do? Use your head, Jordache. We had a deal, remember?'

His eyes roamed over the magnificent view of the deep gorge ahead, the scatterin' of pine-trees and the new growth, the fast-flowin' river and its ripplin' whitewater rapids and the sheer beauty of the untamed wilderness. Not that he or his men considered the view. All they wanted was to lay their hands on the chests of gold bars.

Then he turned to me. 'How do we get down there?'

I shrugged. 'How else? You climb down like I did.'

'It's impossible! How could one man manage to lower several chests of gold bars?'

'I used my head, Jordache. It can be done.'

I remembered the long hard struggle I'd had, but then time was on my side. I'd constructed a crude basket which took one chest and lowered it after I'd gone down and reconnoitred the cave I'd spied earlier. It had been a dreary business of lowerin' a chest and climbin' down to stow it and then climbin' up again to let down another. I was younger and lithe in those days but at the end of the process I'd been tuckered out and had lain alongside the last chest for several hours before blockin' up the entrance to the cave.

As I saw it, no one could ever have visited that cave; the chests would be there still waitin' to be moved again. All we had to do was tie a rope and make a sling at the end of it and then, with one man at the bottom and one at the top to control the rope, the chests would soon be lifted.

I wondered where Luke was. I hoped he was hangin' in there waitin' for my signal, for I knew just when the time would be right to make my move.

First though, I made a stipulation that Amy was to remain at the top of the cliff, so Jordache detailed a man to watch her. Good, I thought. One less for me to worry about, for I knew Luke would dispose of him and spirit Amy away. At least she would be safe.

Then came the great climb down which was more difficult than even Jordache had imagined, for the cliff and the light skim of soil were slippy with the constant wet. One man slipped behind me and I turned quickly as if to reach

51

out a hand to stop him slidin' but I gave him an
extra push and he flailed his arms and plunged
screamin' into the fast-flowin' water below.

Another scumbag off my back!

Jordache was a bit white about the gills when
at last we reached the bottom. I noticed his
hands shakin' and I grinned to myself. The old
sport was nothin' but a hollow shitbag!

I led the way slowly, puttin' one foot in front
of the other and feelin' each rock to see if it
would hold. I didn't want to end up in the river
after all the tribulation. I had to be strong and
ready for whatever occurred. I was thinkin' of
Luke's dynamite. I wondered if he would
remember my signal as to when to come in with
the dynamite. I also wanted to be ready to take
cover if there was any such thing.

I came to the place where I knew the cave
was. It should have been a specially built cairn
of stones. I couldn't find it and I had a feelin' of
panic. Surely I couldn't have mistaken the location? Where there should have been a pile of
rocks to guard the entrance of a cave was now a
mass of scrub.

I moved in like a madman and began tearin'
the thick branches apart. Jordache, almost
breathin' down my neck, grabbed my shoulder.

'What the hell's the matter with you?' he yelled in my ear. I glared at him.

'Something's wrong! There should have been a cairn of stones …'

He slapped me and my head snapped back. The blow cleared my head. I shook it, givin' me time to think.

Then Jordache shoved me aside and began to slash at the thick scrub with his Bowie knife. I let him get on with it. I was wonderin' if the unexpected had happened and someone had stumbled across the cache. If that was the case then I could kiss my life goodbye.

Two of the men behind him helped with the slashin' and soon the loose foliage was bein' thrown down into the river to be swept away.

Then the cave openin' was exposed just as I remembered. It was not quite high enough for a man to walk in upright. I remembered I'd had to bend nearly double to enter, but once inside I could stand upright.

As I recalled, I visualised the long cave that seemed to go far back into the cliffside. I had not explored it all for all I wanted was a hidin' place for the gold.

I remembered it had a smooth sandy floor….

Jordache bent double and stepped inside

followed by the two men. I heard his roar and I ducked down and entered too.

It was then I got a shock. The cave was bare with just a sprinklin' of rubble and a coatin' of dried mud coverin' what once had been sand.

I stared stupidly. That was the aftermath of a landslide when flood water comes rushin' down over hard dry ground. Jordache's fist caught my jaw and I cannoned off the slimy rock wall.

'You bastard! This cave's an outlet for flood water! Was this the place you stashed that gold? Answer truthfully or I'll leave your bones to rot here!'

'Yes, I swear it! On Amy's life, I swear it!'

He gave me a long hard glance and then nodded.

'I believe you and you were a fool! If you'd taken time to look around you would have realized that this place acted as a drain! So ...' he paused, then he said slowly, 'those chests would be swept into the river! If the force was strong enough to sweep away your pile of rocks at the cave's mouth, then the chests could have gone down and because they were heavy not travelled far before sinkin' to the bottom. Mebbe we should take a look at the water below.'

'And who's qualified amongst us to go into

that river to take a look?' I asked as if I couldn't read the answer in his eyes.

His face loomed close to mine. I could smell his breath. He'd been eatin' garlic.

'Who else, buddy, but you? You brought us here. You make good your promise or else ...' he cocked his head as if listenin' and then nodded at a grinnin' Danny. 'You get yourself back up there and bring down the filly.' Then he levelled his gun at me as I made an involuntary movement. 'One false move, Starkey and I'll blow you to Kingdom Come, so get that rotten body of yours in that water and start lookin' for sign. Right now!'

There was a note in his voice that made me realize he was at the end of his rope, so I dived in and the cold mountain water closed over me. It was a shock to the old heart but I gasped and floundered until I got my footin' and began to move downstream, lookin' for any sign of rotten wood or a gleam of gold. I figured that after all this time, if those chests had hurtled down with the slurry and water from that underground sluice, those gold bars might be spewed all over the bottom of the river and caught up between stones.

It was gonna be mighty hard work lookin'

and already my feet and legs were numbin'. I cursed Jordache under my breath.

Then I heard a gunshot and I dived down into the water, thinking the blast was for me. But as I came up for air I saw a body hit the water and sink. Then up it bobbed rollin' over and over and I realized it was the little runt, Danny. I quickly looked upwards to where he must have fallen from, but apart from some movement from overhangin' greenery I could see nothin'.

But I took heart. It must have been Luke! I turned my back on Jordache and his boys who were now rakin' the bushes with gunfire as if they were plagued by demons.

I wished I had a weapon. I felt naked without the weight of a gun at my side. It was as if I was friendless.

As I watched and ducked, I saw where the firin' was comin' from. So did Jordache, who roared to his men to concentrate on that spot. Then he turned suddenly and loosed off a couple of slugs in my direction. It had just occurred to him that I might cut loose.

I yelped as if he'd hit me and then dived under water and let the current carry me downstream. Then I was clamberin' out, sheddin' water by the gallon. I crawled in the undergrowth and started the agonizing climb up the slippery rocks far beyond where all the mayhem was goin' on.

I reckoned Luke was makin' a good play. I was seein' the boy in a new light. He wasn't such an inexperienced fighter after all. I hoped Amy would keep her head down. I must get to them. I felt as if my heart was goin' to bust outta my chest. It had been a long time since I'd exerted myself in that way.

But I climbed high enough, I judged, then I bellied my way through the undergrowth. As I struggled forward I heard a coupla screams and the plop of bodies as they hit the whitewater, to be washed out into the middle of the river and hurtled downstream.

Then I was whistlin' and hootin' to warn Luke I was comin' at a fair lick. I bust through the undergrowth and found them both. Amy was kneelin' down and loadin' up Luke's spare guns as fast as she could and Luke was blazin' away like all getout!

He grinned at me and pointed to the assorted hardware that Amy was attendin' to.

'Forget the guns. What about the dynamite?' I barked at him. He gestured to a pack on the ground beside him, not interruptin' his firepower.

'I daren't use it.' Wasn't sure where you were. But now we can give 'em a real sorting out.'

There were screams and yells below. Luke sure was a crack shot when the need arose. Quickly I pulled out three sticks of dynamite and tried to light the first one. I cursed as my lucifers refused to spark because of the humidity. My hands suddenly trembled. I was exhausted and it was comin' all over me in waves.

Luke glanced at me sharp and thrust his gun into my hand.

'Keep blazin' away, Pop,' – he always called me Pop – 'it don't matter if you miss but just keep 'em occupied and I'll see to the dyno.' Quickly and calmly he took over.

He lit the first fuse, stood countin' and then arced it over the ledge. It fell true and sweet in front of the rocks below where Jordache and his men crouched.

There was an ear-shattering bang and a spout of water flew up into the air like a geyser. With it went mud and rocks and I saw at least two flailin' bodies, all bloodied, disappear amongst broken trees. Those bodies would never be shovelled up to be buried.

I hoped to God that Jordache had had it but I

heard him screamin' to the rest of the men to take cover.

Then Luke threw the second stick. It landed on the edge of the river. This time I was ready for it and threw myself on Amy who was shiverin'.

'It's all right, love,' I shouted in her ear. She would never have heard me otherwise. Then I felt something strike the back of my calf and later I realised that I'd had a bit of muscle gouged out by a sharp rock. At the time it seemed like a bee-sting.

The third stick went further along the river-bank. Luke was just gettin' into his stride and enjoyin' hisself. Then something special happened. There was a mighty roar and a whole mass of loose rocks shot upwards like cannon-balls from a cannon.

Those mighty rocks all about a size reminded me ... I crawled away to see if my fool notion was not as impossible as it seemed.

Then I saw the great hole that was a cave left behind and I sucked in my breath. Surely it wasn't possible? But it was. That second cave held the gold. I'd made a mistake in the beginning. There were caves all along that gorge and the river had gouged out its own path over thousands of years.

Dimly I was aware of the aftermath of the third explosion. It seemed there was no more firin', no more opposition. Whoever was still alive was gettin' out fast....

I stumbled my way towards the new cave. I had to *know*! My legs trembled and I was just about all in for my heart was goin' like a trip-hammer.

I heaved myself up to the ledge where the cave was and half-crawled inside. I stood upright and, adjustin' my eyes to the gloom, I looked about for any traces of chests. There at the back, still stacked as I'd left them, were six boxes.

I whooped with delight and tried to smash one of them open just to glimpse those gold bars. Then a slug came pingin' off a juttin' outcrop of rock, ricochetin' past my ear and soundin' like an angry hornet.

I fell to the ground, part instinct and part shock, then I rolled into the gloom. I cursed for I'd dropped my own gun in the suddenness of it all.

Then I raised my head and saw the figure of Jordache fillin' the openin'. I'd hoped Luke's onslaught might have wiped him out but there he was, as large as life and lookin' mighty grim as he let blaze. I counted four shots. I wondered whether it had been a full load. I couldn't afford a wrong guess.

I played possum and after a long pause, he cautiously stepped inside. I dived for his ankles before he could adjust his eyesight to the darkness. It was a slight advantage but I needed every advantage I could get.

He fell with a crash and I heard the wind gustin' out of him like a leaky balloon. Then I was on him goin' for his throat. I summoned up every ounce of my flaggin' strength to squeeze his air-passages. He fought back. God how he did fight! Those mighty arms and hands tore at me, drawin' blood.

He went for my eyes and I had to loosen my hold on his throat and crack his head against the rock floor.

He heaved and I sailed over him. Then he was on top of me and I was cursin' and frothin' at the mouth and reckonin' I was about done.

We fought like two cats in a sack and all the time I was conscious of dribs and drabs of earth and rock tricklin' down from the roof, no doubt disturbed by the gun explosions.

But Jordache filled my world at that time. I concentrated on him, my breath comin' harshly through my open mouth and my heart poundin' fit to jump out of my body.

Sweat poured from us both. I can still smell the musky odour in my nightmares. Our hands were slimy with it so that we had trouble gettin' to grips.

He caught me a bouncer on my chin and I would have been flung from him if I hadn't seen it comin' a split second before it landed, but I took the power of it on my neck and shoulder. I kicked out and caught his thigh and he screamed and flung himself on me thinkin' to wind me with his weight. I rolled free and he hit the ground and I gave him double-kidney punches that made him howl like a banshee.

Then we were bitin' and gougin' and kickin' and all the while all I could see was a red haze. I felt no pain. That came later.

Then I saw my gun and tried to reach it. He saw what I was after and shook me off like a dog shakes a rat. His reach was longer than mine and he snatched up the gun, his breathin' ragged and wild. I dived as he tried to hold the gun steady and when the gun went off I was foldin' myself up small behind a jagged lump of rock.

That was what saved me, along with his hesitation, for when the explosion came, the whole of the cave roof seemed to collapse and dirt and rock spewed down and Jordache disappeared before my very eyes. One minute he was there, shootin' to kill and the next he was bein' covered by a mound of rocks.

I couldn't believe it! There sure must be someone up there lookin' down and bettin' on the right guy, I thought stupidly.

Then I turned around and except for a smatterin' of rock, the six chests were still intact.

The openin' of the cave was nearly closed with dirt. I could still see a streak of light, but I was too far gone to try and shift that debris by hand. I sank down, thankin' whoever was up there for leavin' a smidgeon of air to reach me.

After that all went black. I don't know how long I was lyin' there but I was shaken awake by Luke. He had somehow located me and had torn down the rocks and come lookin'. I was never so glad to see anyone in my life.

I sat up, still confused.

'What happened?'

Luke thrust a bottle in my hand.

'Have a snort. You nearly got yourself buried alive. I heard the gun goin' off but I couldn't find you straight away. But there's an almighty great crack up yonder and a whole heap of cliff has fallen away. I reckon the dynamite weakened the whole river-bank and the gunshots just sent the whole lot crashin' down.'

'So Jordache has had it?'

Luke's eyebrows raised.

'It was him was it? I wondered. Couldn't see no sign of his body when I looked the men over. I reckoned he had gone down the river or got away. So he came after you?'

'Yeah, took me by surprise.' The whiskey tasted good and it brought all my senses back. I shuddered as the liquor warmed my guts but what made me shudder even more was the last sight of Jordache. I wouldn't want any enemy of mine to suffer like he would suffer before he died. Better be blown away than left to suffocate.

I nodded to the chests.

'There they are, Luke. Six chests of gold bars belongin' to the Government in Washington.' I took another drink and now I was feelin' pissed, what with fightin' an' all.

Luke gave me an old-fashioned look.

'How come you've known about them all these years?'

That was the question I'd dreaded. I hesitated. Luke was a smart boy. I'd have to make it good.

'I was with the military and one of the guards,' I lied. 'We were jumped by a gang of cut-throats and Jordache was the army officer who betrayed the whereabouts of the wagon-train and what it was carryin'. He was in cahoots with the gang boss. I kept quiet because I knew that if I didn't, I'd be cat's-meat.'

'Well, how come Jordache didn't know the location and came after you?'

Goddamn the boy for bein' too smart! 'Well now, it's quite a long story.'

'We've got time,' Luke said brusquely, 'neither of us is goin' anywhere.'

I coughed. He was gettin' uppity. I wasn't havin' that.

'Look, young feller, we've no time to jaw. If Amy's up there on her own, we've gotta get to her before she begins to worry.'

Luke nodded. 'Right, but remember I'm wantin' some answers. In the meanwhile we'll have to get those chests hauled topsides and we'll have to find Jordache's bunch of hosses to freight 'em away. After all, we've got to return 'em to the authorities.'

I gulped and choked on my next drink.

'Do we have to?'

'Have to what?'

'Return 'em to the authorities? I thought' ... I stopped when I saw Luke's shocked face. He was too goddamn straight.

'You thought what?'

I shrugged. He could be an explosive young devil when roused. I reckoned he was still wet behind the ears and nursed too many ideals. He hadn't gone through the war like I had. He'd learn. But now I didn't want no argy-bargy. I wasn't up to it. I let it go.

'Nothin'. Just it would be a mighty trek haulin' all that lot back to Washington.'

'We could haul it back to the ranch and I can report it to the county marshal who would know what to do.'

I shrugged again.

'Not what I want. It's what's the right thing to do. Mebbe there'll be a reward' – now his eyes gleamed – 'we could split it and I could marry Amy and mebbe buy my own place!'

I gave a lop-sided grin. There we were only the two of us with our hands on nearly a half a million dollars' worth of gold bars and he was goin' all lyrical about mebbe pickin' up a few measly dollars as a reward! I could have spit!

But I didn't. I went along with it for peace's sake. Time to do a bit of persuadin' when it was all over. Now we had to get those chests hauled up to the cliff top and find those hosses of Jordache's men. There was the risk of the chests bein' rotten after all these years and seein' them there gold bars bounce right back into the river.

Hell! Luke had no idea of the problems ahead.

I stopped his ramblin's pronto.

'Stop dreamin' boy and get yourself braced. We're gonna shift those chests and find out if they'll take the strain of liftin'.'

'Eh? Are we startin' right now?'

'Yeah, the sooner the better. We got Amy up there all on her own. Remember? We look 'em over and then you'll shin up there and tie our ropes together and fasten them good and let 'em down. Meanwhile I'll bring out a chest and tie it up if the planks aren't rotten. While you haul it up I'll bring out another one. Right?'

'What if the chests *are* rotten?'

'Then we make a basket-net, dolt, and haul them up as best as we can.'

'But how do we carry 'em away?'

'We'll figure that out when we get 'em all up.

With a bit of luck and if that cave was dry most of the time the chests won't give.'

Luke gave me a tight-lipped nod. He picked up a chest, carried it outside and I dragged another one outside. My muscles were no match to his. At least I could get a much-needed rest while he did the climbin'.

It seemed no time at all till he was shoutin' down at me.

'Hoy there, are you asleep?'

'D'you think I'm a moron?'

'What's a moron?'

'Never you mind. Just get on with that rope.'

'All set, so watch yourself.'

I made a grab as it snaked down. I pulled at it to make sure it was really tied fast.

'Is Amy all right?' I yelled up to him.

'Yeah, fried some bacon. She wants to know if we should lower some down.'

'A good idea. Have we another rope? It might be handy.'

'Yeah, comin' down and she's wrapped the bacon in a hunk of bread and rolled it in a leaf so watch out for it.'

I ate the bread and bacon as I tied up the first chest. It didn't seem to have rotted so I took a chance and I prayed as it swung against the rock-face on its way up. I would have died a death if the whole thing had collapsed and I'd have to watch those gleamin' gold bars splash into that cursed river.

It seemed an age before Luke shouted that the chest was safe. I breathed a sigh of relief.

The second chest got hung up on a juttin' piece of rock and we had to pull and then lower the rope several times to free it. Once the chest hit the rock with a jarring crash and I was sure we would lose it and the contents. But no, the chest held and both Luke and Amy hauled it up between them.

Now I was in a black sweat and feelin' drained. I could have lain down amongst pig shit and slept. But I carried on until it was too dark to see and it would have been risky to move the last two boxes.

I shouted up that that was the last for today and we'd try again as soon as dawn broke. In the meantime, Luke would look after Amy and I would doss down where I fell....

I was all aches and pains when I awakened from a brief doze. Age was catchin' up and I missed my comfortable bed.

I hollered up to Luke who peered over, lookin' half asleep. I suspected him and her hadn't passed all night in sleep. But then of course they were young and passions run high and who was I to object? I would have done the same as him at his age.

'All set for the next chest?' I hollered.

'Right. Here we go!' Luke gathered all his new-found strength and made short work of the haulin'.

It was with the last chest that trouble came. Luke yanked at the rope and pulled hard. I watched it swing into the air and suddenly it was comin' down fast. The last thing I knew it was comin' straight at me.

Luke said afterwards that it hit me fair and square and that I was lucky it didn't knock me into the river. He'd dragged up the chest with Amy's help though she'd screamed blue murder when it happened.

Then he'd climbed down to see to me. He said I was out cold.

I don't remember him tying me with the rope and I don't remember bein' lifted a few feet or even fallin' again when the rope was cut.

But I did wake up when the gun went off and Luke hurtled to the ground and winded me as he landed on top of me.

I looked up all bemused, and saw Jordache

lookin' down at us and grinnin' like a wolf that's just killed its prey, but what really struck terror into my heart was realizing that Amy was in the grip of that monster again.

'Thanks for doin' all the dirty work, Starkey! Sorry about that boy. He was a real good worker. But now I've got to go. We've gotta lot of travellin' to do!' With that he emptied what was once one of my Peacemakers down at us, the slugs chippin' lumps out of the rock all around.

But he mustn't have been in a mood for killin' for he only hit me once and that was a lump out of one ear. I could live with that.

Then they were gone and I groaned as I turned Luke over. He was still alive, thank God. I'd never prayed to God so much as I had this last few days. I think it helped. I know it did.

FIVE

The next few hours were a nightmare. Luke had taken a slug through the shoulder, narrowly missin' bone and blastin' out from the other side, so he was lyin' in a welter of blood. At least I didn't have to poke around diggin' out no lead.

I used his bandanna and some strips off my shirt to make pads and bound him up tightly to stop that dreadful flow. It suddenly came to me as I worked over him that to me, Luke was the son I never had. My hands trembled with the knowledge. It was as if I'd just found him only to lose him. I listened anxiously for signs of breathin' or a faint heartbeat. For a few moments he put all thoughts of Amy out of my mind.

Then I was relieved to detect the faint beat of

his heart, for I thought the crashin' down might have done what the slug failed to do. But he was alive, thank God.

The next problem was gettin' him up that steep cliff; my old body was not in the best of shape. The rope which was actually two ropes strung together had been cut and lay coiled beside us.

I looked up that cliff and it seemed to go on for ever. Then I noticed that here and there were juttin' ledges where a feller might rest before goin' on. Mebbe there was a way after all.

I swilled whiskey into Luke's mouth. At first it was a waste of good liquor soakin' into the ground; then he shuddered and moaned and I took heart. His eyes flickered open and he stared at me as I squatted beside him.

'Wha ... what happened?' he whispered, throat dry. I gave him a quick nip of whiskey and his tongue licked over his lips like it was an elixir of life.

'That bastard Jordache must have been born lucky! Somehow he got outta that cave and crawled up some air-pocket or somethin'.

'But what happened to me ...' he paused, then said, eyes wide open, 'what happened to Amy?'

I didn't want to tell him but he guessed.

'The bastard took her, didn't he?' He struggled on to one elbow. I shoved him gently back down flat.

'Easy now, boy, don't set those holes bleedin' again. I've had hell's own job to stop 'em drainin' you dry.'

'Never mind me, what about her!' His hand on my arm was amazingly strong for a feller who'd been shot and fallen so far.

I nodded reluctantly. 'He cut the rope, and took her and I expect the gold has gone with him. We're out on a limb, boy.'

'We're goin' after her,' Luke said between clenched teeth. Every movement must have hurt bad.

'I am, but you're gonna rest up. You're in no fit state to ride after them. I'll take the rest of the dynamite and all the ammo I can carry plus your rifle. I'll leave you your guns and then I'll come back for you.'

'You're mighty confident you can catch 'em up! You, an old man, nearly past it....'

I stiffened angrily. No need to rub my nose in it. I think he saw the anger in my eyes because he said softly, 'No offence, Starkey, but you *are* gettin' on.'

That was true but he didn't know I had a rod of steel down my back that was still there even though the last years had been soft for me. Besides, I had a hell of an incentive. That bloated lump of pig shit had taken my child. Nobody could do that and live.

'I'm comin' with you,' Luke said quietly, but forcefully.

I knew it was no good reasonin' with him. He'd made his mind up.

'We haven't got up this cliff yet and we don't know if we've hosses. It would take at least three to carry the chests and he might have driven off the rest before he left.'

Luke groaned and took another slug of whiskey. I looked upwards and thought it was no good messin' about. I might as well get started. So I coiled the rope around me and began to climb. I knew what I was goin' to do. I'd get to the top and make the rope fast and then pick out a route, takin' in all those ledges I saw. We'd rest at each one and gradually make our way upwards.

It was a hell of a climb and my muscles and joints were screamin' well before I got there. I had to rest. As I expected there were no signs of hosses. The bastard had done a good job.

Then, when I got my wind back and my legs felt less like jelly, I took a walk. I was curious about how Jordache had come out of that cave alive.

I soon found my answer. The whole side of the cliff had cracked open and the tunnels underneath were like a rabbit warren. It was easy to see how Jordache had clawed his way to the surface. I reckoned he would never be so lucky again.

I found a safe anchorage for the rope, then takin' a deep breath, began the descent. It wasn't easy what with the wind that got up and the swift-flowin' river below which made me dizzy to look at.

Nevertheless I landed beside him at last. He looked a bit grey but awake and alert.

'How you feel?' I asked, concerned and wondering whether I'd ever get him slung upright to start the climb.

He grunted and tried to heave himself up on his legs.

'Hold your hosses,' I said, 'I'm not God Almighty. I need a rest and I've got the last of the grub in my jacket. We gotta eat to keep up our strength.'

He ate like it was poison so I finished off

what he was leavin'. I needed my belly filled even though it was stale bread and cold bacon. Then we both took a share of what was left in the whiskey bottle and we were as ready as we would ever be.

I took a deep breath and heaved him upright. He swayed a little and I knew he was hurt more bad than I'd realized.

But I got him climbin' slowly and I took his weight and what with watchin' my feet and hand-holds and supportin' him I had a merry old time. I was soon in a black sweat.

I was glad when we got to the first ledge and rested. It wasn't much over twelve feet from the ground but it felt like for ever.

We rested some and then went on. We did that right up that cursed cliff. My muscles screamed for rest so I don't know what agonies he went through but he was tight-lipped and apart from some cussin', didn't utter a word.

We lay winded on top of the cliff. At that time I wouldn't have cared if a whole Indian tribe came down on us. The only one who would have got a real reaction outta me would have been Jordache and he was long gone.

I tried not to think of Amy and what he might be puttin' her through. I concentrated on thinkin' of skinnin' him alive and cookin' his balls and stuffin' them down his throat. The anger in me counteracted the extreme exhaustion.

Then I saw that Luke was comfortable and I knew I had to cast around and see if there was at least one horse grazin' nearby.

I was lucky. My hoss, which I'd had for a number of years and was pampered more than cowboy hosses usually are, had not strayed far. He was croppin' the green lush grass which grew plentifully in that wet place. Beside him was one of the scumbags' nags, not a very well-cared for specimen, probably one that Jordache looked over and considered cat's-meat.

I whistled. My hoss raised his head, ears twitchin', and nickered and came trottin' to me. The strange hoss looked up and followed and when I walked back to Luke with my hoss the other followed quietly.

We had transport again.

Luke didn't settle well on the bony nag but that nag was better than nothin'. We weren't goin' at speed anyway. As long as we could move and mebbe cast around and find some sign of a string of hosses movin' out was all that mattered.

It took some time to find the tracks of the

milling bunch of hosses. They'd kicked and flung a bit, for none were packhorses and those chests would be a mite hard to stack aboard a protestin' hoss and fasten down. He had three hosses to hump the chests on to. So perhaps the bastard wouldn't be too far ahead.

I reckoned he would fasten each hoss nose to tail and lead 'em off that way with Amy tied to her hoss and him holdin' her reins. It would take all his skill to make good time. I cheered up. The bastard wouldn't be too far in front of us.

We found his trail. The mishmash of hoof-prints suddenly spread out. He was workin' his way south, probably makin' for Mexico. I would have done that in his position.

I looked at Luke. He was lookin' white and drawn but still perky.

'You be up to it, Luke?' I asked. I didn't want the boy suddenly quittin' on me and fallin' from that old nag. If he did, I would sure as hell leave him behind, no matter how much of a son he was to me. I reckoned he should know this. I coughed. It wasn't easy what I was about to say. 'Luke, no matter what happens, I think of you as a son. You know that don't you?'

'Yeah, sort of. What are you tryin' to say, Starkey?'

'Well now, no offence but if you can't keep up....' I hesitated but he jumped in before I could finish what I was about to say. He was sharp was that boy.

'You'll leave me behind. That's it, isn't it? That's what you're tryin' to say?'

'Yes. I'm thinkin' of Amy, boy. She'll be in no trouble while they're travellin'. It'll take him all his time to control those hosses and her, but at night....'

'Yeah, I've thought of that, Starkey, and I wouldn't want to hold you back, not that I intend to. No sir! I might not look at m'best but I'm gonna keep up all the way!'

I nodded. The kid had grit.

We moved out, pretty certain on which way they would go and even kept up a good pace until well after sundown, until the clouds covered the half moon. Then we quit and rested up until dawn. I made sure we both ate well before movin' on, as we might not be able to stop for another meal until the day was far gone.

Luke's nag was a slow mover. Must have been ridden hard for a long time to be in such a poor condition. But he was better than nothin' and my hoss couldn't have rid double over that harsh country.

We were now away from the lush greenery and we had to look out for water-holes or mebbe a tiny stream but though we saw watercourses, they were mainly dried up and only in use durin' floodings.

We saw signs of deer and the droppin's of big cats but nothin' near enough to shoot at. Far away ahead of us we could see buzzards wheelin' high in the sky. Somethin' must be dead and they were waitin' for the predator to leave his kill so they could move in. Fleetingly I wondered what it might be.

Three hours later I found out what that carcass was. It was a hoss and there wasn't much left of it, only bits of meat on the skeleton. I reckoned it was one of Jordache's hosses.

The saddle had been stripped from it, as had all the rest of the harness and I saw some way from it the remains of a splintered chest.

So that was it. The horse had slipped and broken a front leg and the chest had bounced and broken open. I reckoned Jordache would have quite a job stashin' ten gold bars in any available saddle-bag on those frisky hosses. It must have set him back quite a few hours.

It was all to our good. We were on the right track and not too far behind. We moved on.

Even Luke was beginning to look more cheerful.

The night had fallen and the moon was risin' when we finally caught up with them. First we smelled smoke and the faint aroma of coffee. The bastard was confident enough to be careless. He would expect to have left a couple of corpses behind. Well, he would soon find out his mistake!

We turned our hosses and camped well out of range of our hosses nickerin' for the others to hear. We didn't want to alert Jordache before we were ready for him.

I told Luke very firmly that he was to rest while I did a bit of scoutin' around. It paid off to be patient and find out all that was needed to know before any conflict. It was the same in the army or leadin' a gang. Make sure of the terrain, the strength of the opposition and any weaknesses that might show up.

Of course this was a piddlin' operation to what I'd known in the past, but I had to know exactly where Amy was and where he would be likely to be and just where the camp was and how it was surrounded by trees, cliffs or a bluff. It all counted.

I moved in a wide circle, closin' in as I did so.

Funny how old habits come back. I moved Indian-fashion, puttin' a foot down carefully and avoidin' dry twigs that would crack like thunderclaps in the still of the night.

Then as the smell of coffee and smoke became stronger, I bellied down and moved forward inch by inch. That was when I had a confrontation with a coiled up sidewinder shelterin' under a rock. I nearly up and yelled, but I grabbed it by the back of the neck before it could rear up. I reckoned it was as surprised as me. It thrashed a bit but I severed its head with my knife and threw it into the scrub. I shuddered a bit. I never could abide snakes.

Then I was watchin' the two of them. Amy was sittin' cowed by the fire. I saw that her ankles were bound. She wasn't goin' anywhere. He was crouched near the flames, fryin' what smelled like venison in my old black pan. The bastard wasn't even usin' his own!

Trouble was he was right close to her, that if I'd shot him and missed I might have hit her. I cursed inwardly. It was the perfect moment to take him before he knew I was there and I couldn't do it.

It was as if he instinctively figured that he had to use her body to protect himself. I suppose years ago I would have done the self-same thing.

At least Amy didn't look as if Jordache had been playin' games with her. He would have too much on his plate to think of dallyin'. He would reckon to have her when they were both safe in Mexico. That gold was far too important to get sidetracked by a woman.

I eased my way backwards. Luke would have to be in on this. He would have to take charge of Amy while I took on Jordache. I reckoned the best time would be when they turned in. Jordache must sleep sometime.

I made my way back to Luke and explained in whispers what had happened. He agreed with me, that we couldn't rush in heedlessly, with slugs flyin', until we could get Amy away. Luke was impatient to get after her but saw the sense of waitin' until they'd turned in for the night.

We both chewed on lumps of cold fried bacon and drank water from our canteens. I needed liquor badly but we were out of whiskey and coffee was out of the question. We waited, tensed up and twitchy.

Then, when I thought the time was right, we both wriggled our way through the undergrowth to watch and assess what Jordache was up to.

The bastard was still awake. We watched him drinkin' and starin' at Amy's swaddled-up figure in a blanket. I knew what was goin' through the dirty scumbag's mind. He was itchy and only the thought of his back bein' vulnerable when he was on the job was what was stoppin' him, even though it was unlikely that anyone was around for at least a hundred miles.

Still, he could reckon there could be other dangers. Lone cowboys or big cats, attracted by his fire. Cautious, Ike Jordache was takin' no chances.

We crouched in the scrub until I got the cramps and had to belly away fast to get away to stand up and stretch my heel to relieve the agony. I cursed my advancin' age.

Then I heard gunfire and cussin' like all get-out, I raced back to find Luke kneelin' and aimin' at Jordache who held a smokin' gun in one hand and Amy by the other.

She was strugglin' hard.

'You fool! What happened?' I gasped.

'He suddenly dived for her. Jesus, Starkey, I had no choice. I think I winged him. He yelped as he blazed back at me, but he grabbed her before I could plug him!' He breathed hard and sweat poured from his brow; he was sure goin' through it, seein' his girl in the hands of a monster like Jordache.

'We've lost the advantage of surprise,' I said bitterly. 'At least you could have waited until he started undressin' her!'

Luke stared at me, his eyes dangerous in the light of the moon.

'She's your daughter, Starkey! You're talkin' about Amy! How could I wait after that bastard got his vile hands on her?'

I sighed. The impulsiveness of youth! Amy wouldn't have been hurt, only frightened, mebbe, and he could have stole up and blasted the back of Jordache's head. Unpleasant for Amy but she would have got over it.

Now we had a standoff.

'Jordache! Do you hear me? It's Starkey. You let my girl go and you can get to hell out of it with the gold. We won't follow you.'

'Like hell you won't!' Jordache bellowed back. 'You think I'm a fool? She's my ace in the hole. One wrong move from you, Starkey and I let daylight into her head!'

'You're a dead man if you do, and you won't

die easy,' I yelled back, blood boilin' and ravin' mad. 'You're a no-win loser, Jordache! You can't fight us off and keep a hold on her *and* control those hosses of yours!'

For a moment there was silence and I guessed he was thinkin' of his options. Then I heard him laugh, and my blood ran cold. What was the evil son of a bitch cookin' up now?

I didn't believe my ears when at last he gave mouth. I felt rather than saw Luke move angrily by my side, his wound obviously painin' him.

'You remember Moll, Starkey? How you took her from me and laughed in my face when the bitch ditched me for you?'

Moll? I vaguely remembered some little whore we'd come across in some bawdy house when we'd been holing up before we pulled the bullion raid. It had been a matter of cunnin' tactics to take Jordache's woman, he bein' an army officer an' all that. Me and my boys had been layin' up ready for the big time, and hidin' out near the fort where Jordache was based, so that we could meet and confer. Moll had been a challenge. She was no great shakes in bed or out of it. It was just the fact that she could be taken from Jordache. Malicious hijinks on my part. He could have had her back next day, but at that time he'd been too proud....

'Yeah, I remember,' I shouted back. 'What become of her?'

'I don't know and I don't care, but you took her from me. Now I'm takin' your daughter, Starkey, in exchange. How's that for a laugh?'

For a minute I was stunned. If he hadn't pulled Amy partly behind a boulder with just enough showin' to make it plain that she was bein' held, I should have rushed him there and then.

'Moll wasn't worth the trouble you'll be in if you don't give her up, Jordache,' I managed to grate out between clenched teeth. 'What about that gold? It would buy you a whole heap of women!'

'Didn't you know? I made me a pile when I broke jail. I'd rather leave you the gold and take your girl. I'm what those in Washington would call a philanthropist. You can have it in exchange for her!'

'Goddamn you, Jordache! Quit playin' games! You'd never give up a fortune in gold! It's against your nature!'

I motioned to Luke to start movin' around while I kept the bastard talkin'. I never once believed a word he said, but I was wrong. I kept needlin' him, hopin' he would get angry and try somethin' rash and I would be ready.

In the meanwhile, I knew Luke, wounded as he was, would finally get around the back of him and then we'd have him cold.

But the wily son of a bitch only answered in curt phrases and all the while he must have been gettin' ready to move out.

Suddenly, during a lengthy tirade of threats on my part, I suddenly heard his reckless laugh and the sound of a horse crashin' through the scrub. The bastard must have caught a sound of Luke's clumsy approach.

I leapt to my feet and emptied my guns in the direction they were travellin', suddenly oblivious to the fact I might have hit Amy. God forgive me for that, but I was so mad I couldn't reason.

Then Luke lurched out of the bushes, and I knew we were alone. He was cryin' like a baby. I didn't blame him. I wanted to cry myself.

'We'll get him yet, Luke. He hasn't seen the last of us! We'll foller him to hell and back if necessary!'

Luke just looked at me. I never saw such devastation on a feller's face before, like it was on Luke's. He didn't answer but fell to the ground and lay motionless.

Pity for him and fear for my girl choked me up, but I vowed then and there, I'd make it up to both of them if we all came out of this alive.

SIX

We didn't move out from the camp for three days. Luke was out of his head all the first night and all the next day. When I stripped the makeshift bandages from his wounds, it was as I feared, the tell-tale signs of blood-poisonin' was there. All around the wounds the flesh was red and angry showin' the first hint of purple which would spread rapidly into his bloodstream if I didn't do somethin' about it. Already the wounds were suppuratin' a thick yeller pus and the smell was vile.

My stomach quaked but I knew what had to be done. I raked the embers of the fire and tossed on more wood to make a good blaze and all the while Luke tossed and moaned and mumbled words I couldn't understand. He was right off his head. I filled the coffee-pot with water and boiled it and while it boiled I searched around for something to tear up for clean wrappin'. It was then, when I looked in the saddle-bags of the horses Jordache had left behind, that I found the loose bars of gold stashed away. It looked as if he'd thrown out everythin' to make way for the gold. There was nothin' to salvage otherwise.

If it hadn't been so serious I could have laughed at the irony of it. We had two pack-horses carryin' four chests and one horse carryin' one. Amy must have ridden one of the extra mounts, and every saddle-bag was stuffed with the extra gold bars and nothin' else, while here we were in dire need of extra food and anythin' I could lay my hands on to bind up Luke's wounds when I'd done the business.

But I found a clean shirt of Luke's. He was more particular than I was. I never thought about settin' out with a change of clothes. My shirts were usually worn until they fell off my back.

Luke's shirt was a godsend. I tore the sleeves out and put them one at a time into the coffee-pot and boiled them. While they boiled I tore the rest of the shirt into strips and tied several pieces together, The rest I was goin' to use to clean up the wounds when I'd finished what had to be done.

Then I found two forked sticks and dug them well into the ground. I put a third branch across and laid the sleeves over them to dry.

Then I drew a long hard breath. I couldn't put it off any longer. I took my Bowie knife and I held it in the flames of the fire until I knew there was no chance of any germs on it. I waved it under my nose and felt the heat on my chin and knew I was as ready as I would ever be.

I turned Luke over clumsily. He lay like one dead. Then I plunged the point of the knife into the wound at the back of his shoulder. It sizzled sickeningly but it was cauterized.

He half came round and screamed as I turned him over. Then he fell back and I was able to soak up the new clean blood with some of the rags. I made a pad of one of the sleeves to put on the wound when the time was right.

I cleaned and heated the knife again and did the same with the wound in the front. This time he came around and it was a struggle to hold him down. Again he sank into a dead faint. I was able to clean and staunch the bleedin' before placin' the rolled up sleeve pad into position.

The hard bit was keepin' the pads still as I bound him up with the long bandagin'. I had to make it good so that it wouldn't shift. We had some hard ridin' to do when he was up to it.

I'd done the best I could for him. He'd have two bad scars when they healed, but I knew they *would* heal. Now all I could do was watch over him and fight the fever and wait for him to get his senses back.

That next day was a nightmare. Sometimes he was quiet and sometimes he was fightin' mad and I had to hold him down, but by nightfall he started to sweat and I knew the fever had broken.

He was thirsty and at first I gave him sips of water. Then I soaked some of our small supply of stale bread in water and he swallowed some. Then he asked for coffee and I knew the battle was more than half won.

The third day he could get up and I didn't have to help him piss. He was wobbly on his legs but at least they held him upright. He looked gaunt and his beard was bristly and he smelled of sickness but I knew he was on the mend.

'Luke,' I said, 'we've got to talk. D'you remember anythin' about the gunfight? D'you realize

Jordache took off with Amy and they're ridin' double?'

He looked at me a bit vacantly, his head still muzzy.

'They got away? I remember somethin'. I was firin' and suddenly I felt this godawful pain as if my shoulder was on fire and then nothin' until you were pokin' me with red hot needles.'

'Sorry, son, but I had to do it. You were sufferin' from lead poisonin' and you would have died otherwise.'

'Then I owe you, Starkey.' He looked about him. 'How long have we been here?'

'This is the third day, Luke.'

'And they've got further away. We'll have to make a move, Starkey.' His voice wobbled a little. As I said before, the boy had guts.

'Yeah, I'm afraid so, Luke. We're startin' at daybreak, so you'd better get all the sleep you can.'

I prepared him a bacon sandwich. I didn't eat myself. He noticed but I said I'd eaten earlier. The smell of the bacon made my guts churn but he needed the grub more than I did. Tomorrow, when we started to ride, I would keep a look-out for some game. It was time we had fresh meat.

The dawn came all too soon for Luke. I

hoisted him aboard one of Jordache's extra horses and turned Luke's half-starved nag loose to fend for itself. I used a rope and fastened him on tight. I didn't want him takin' a toss on his wounded shoulder.

During the waiting time I'd been thinking about Jordache and what he would aim to do. He would head for Mexico and probably look up old friends. I knew of some of his old haunts; in our wild days we knew every short cut and every river crossin'. We needed to, for it meant freedom for us who were on the owlhoot trail.

So when we started out I cast around and we followed the faint trail of Jordache's horse. The hoofprints were deep because of the extra weight the horse was carryin'. His right hind hoof was a little misshapen and easy to follow. We rode fast and hard. I wanted to make up the time we'd wasted. His horse would not be able to travel as fast as our two fresh horses could.

Soon, Luke's head rested on his horse's neck. He never complained but that ride must have been hell for him.

We came to several small townships and asked around and found that a man and a woman had passed through. The man had bought a fresh horse and some food, but they'd not stayed the night in town. I reckoned they were in a hurry to cross the border.

Meanwhile, we took advantage of the stops and Luke got his shoulder attended to by a doctor who asked no questions and sold us extra bandages and some smelly ointment for a highly inflated price. I didn't grumble with that. I would have done the same.

At least now we knew Luke's shoulder was on the mend, even though the doctor reckoned the doc who'd cauterized it was a clumsy half-wit. I saw Luke's eyes gleam with amusement and kept my mouth shut. Well, I wasn't a doctor, but I was used to doin' rough-and-ready surgery on anybody who would allow it. At least I had the guts. Some fellers would have just looked at that festerin' mess and left it, with dire consequences.

We cleaned up and shaved and I helped Luke to bathe and dress again and we felt more human. For the first time I had the feelin' we weren't movin' amongst sewerage any more. We could smell the sagebrush, and the scent of pines when we came to a stand of trees was exhilaratin'. You don't know what you're missin' when you stink.

Each day, Luke travelled better. I knew when

to stop for a break; we changed horses frequently but now the horses we were usin' as pack animals were holdin' us back. The animals had sores on their backs from the constant rubbin' of those chests, so finally and reluctantly I decided to bury the lot again and free the horses. We would keep an extra horse each so that we could keep ridin' and not kill our mounts and we would travel as light as possible. I reckoned that in a week we could be within a decent distance of the Red River.

I reckoned Jordache with Amy holdin' him back a little must be only a week or ten days ahead. If we could put a spurt on now that Luke could keep up the pace, we could cross the river not far behind, and once over the border, we could make for all the places that I knew of where Jordache could hang out.

Luke was beginning to give me funny looks. He'd never known that I knew this country like the back of my hand and that it wasn't much different from the days of my youth.

I pondered a long time about comin' clean with him and lettin' him into my secret. My worry was if he would spill everythin' to Amy once all this was over.

I never once thought that things might turn

out wrong and that Luke and I would never see Amy again. I just refused to entertain such ideas. I'm not sure what he thought. We seemed to deliberately keep off the subject of what we would do if we failed....

I knew Jordache and I reckoned that if he thought he'd got away with Amy, he would keep her alive. It would feed his ego to use her. His reasonin' would be that every time he molested her, he would take it as revenge on me and the loss of the gold.

That knowledge was no comfort to me. I hated to think of my sweet Amy sufferin' for what happened between Jordache and me.

My only aim now in life was to see her again, face the bastard and beat shit out of him before I killed him. I wanted to see the fear in his eyes when he looked down that Peacemaker he took off me all those years ago. I wanted him to die slow and hard.

The little town of Santo Domingo was only fifty miles from the Rio Grande. We were in luck. Jordache and Amy had stayed two nights in the small hotel. Their horses had been reshod and the girl had rested up in the bedroom and Jordache had spent the nights boozin' with the fellers in the bar.

We entered the little town quietly, just two drifters comin' into town. I'd found an ideal place to stash the gold and Luke had made a rough sketch on a Wanted poster he'd snitched at the last stop. We left the site lookin' undisturbed. It was a good thing we did as it turned out, we could move fast when needed and it could be a talkin' point if things went wrong with Jordache.

We stayed long enough to have us a good feed, stock up on victuals and shells and get all the information we could on Jordache's plans. I reckoned that when he was tanked up with liquor he would start to brag. He did and for the price of a few beers we got a good idea of where he was headin'.

He was aimin' for the owl-hoot town, Nuevocruz, high in the Mexican hills. I had heard of it years ago but had never been there. It was a cluster of broken-down huts and makeshift tents, the remnants of a once-thrivin' gold town. It had been left deserted when the gold petered out, then taken up by all the wanted men from both Mexico and over the border.

I also knew it was run by a one-time buddy of Jordache. He'd boasted in the old days about his alliance with Big Blond Barney Trevellian. As an army officer, Jordache had tipped off Trevellian as to the whereabouts of caches of arms and ammunition for the army and about the army's plans of attack on many owl-hoot gangs. It had got so bad that Trevellian had been run out of the US and had found a haven in Mexico.

So he was still around. No-one had put a bullet in him yet!

But I had friends of my own in these parts. There were those old buddies who owed me; long standin' debts which now might be paid, if those same buddies were still alive. But the odds were, that even if only half of my one-time contacts were stll drawin' breath, I could outwit Jordache and his old buddy.

Nuevocruz. I reckoned that mebbe now I was gonna see that owl-hoot town and find out whether all the old myths and legends were true.

But I was in a quandary. If I was to ride, straight-backed and chin up, into that nest of hoodlums, I'd have to go in with more than an air of bravado. I'd have to ride in as a success-ful boss-man, a man who when he nodded, had the power of life and death over other men. In short, I had to ride in with all the panache of a known gang-boss, with guns ready to prove I was one of them ...

It meant givin' Luke the low-down on my past life.

It meant castin' aside a veil of respectability which I'd tried hard to cultivate for Amy's sake.

It meant showin' Luke Channing just what kind of man his future father-in-law really was.

I had no idea how Luke would react. It meant peelin' away a skin I never really was entitled to. Luke was a law-abidin' young sheriff, used to dealin' with local drunks and the odd Saturday-night capers. How would he react when he knew that Amy's old man was an original wild man, wanted in several states for robbery and murder too. It was no use glossin' things over, he could check back on all Wanted posters and if he dug deep enough he could still come up with some of the more lurid details of my past life.

I had to take a gamble for Amy's sake. I was still that wild ruthless bastard under the skin, and my mean streak was well to the fore. I'd get that son of a bitch, Jordache, if I had to swing for him.

I must say I was surprised that Luke didn't

blink when I finally got around to tellin' him. We'd tanked up at the bar of the best saloon in Santo Domingo. It was a quiet clean little town of adobe houses and a white church with a tall spire, just a couple of hotels and a few saloons, and a way station for those changin' horses before they rode for the border and the river. There was a reg'lar service to the ford crossing over the Rio Grande. It was the last important stoppin' place before crossin' into Mexico.

The liquor was good and I was ready to tackle Luke. I would know one way or the other when I first opened up to him, whether I should go on alone or whether he would still come with me.

He supped his whiskey as he listened. noddin' every now and then as if some pieces of jigsaw were comin' into place. One of the things that had bothered him was the fact I knew about the stash of gold.

I gave him the lot. I told him about my early life as a kid and how I'd had to survive the best way I could after my folks were killed. I told him about the practice shootin' for hours on end until I could drop a man in ten seconds flat.

He seemed to understand when I said the power grew in me and that when men stepped out of my path, it gave me a great kick. To have powerful older men afraid meant that I was ready to give orders and plan and direct, and the success of those plans and the cash we accumulated so easily was better than goin' with a woman.

'You're not shocked?' I asked him. He grinned and shook his head.

'I've felt somethin' similar myself when I've hunted down an escaped prisoner when helpin' the state-marshal. Figurin' on the prisoner's next move an' bein' successful. Mind you, I've never had the excitement of bein' part of a team on a raid, but it must be mighty exhilaratin', and I've felt the savage urge to kill when I've been in a fight. I think I can understand you, Starkey.' He shook his head. 'I never lost my folks early on, or mebbe I would have grown up different.'

I looked at him squarely in the face. 'You won't tell Amy about all this?'

He reached over and took my hand in his and gave it a squeeze.

'You're the same old Starkey. Amy won't find out from me.'

'Good.' That promise eased the tension in me. I didn't want Amy to know, ever. It had to be a secret between Luke and me.

'What do we do now?' Luke asked.

I gave him it straight. 'Look, I'll not think less of you if you decide to quit. It's goin' to be dangerous. You can turn right round and ride back the way we've come. You have the map. You can go dig up that gold and take it back to Washington and claim the kudos for findin' it and returnin' it to the Treasury. They'll pay a good sum as a reward. They'll be only too glad to have it back.'

Luke pursed his lips and pulled 'em down at the corners.

'What you take me for, Starkey? Some prissy weaklin' or somethin'? I'm sure not lettin' you take that Jordache on your own!'

'I won't be alone. I have friends around these parts.'

'I'm still goin' to be in at the kill. Remember, I've just as much to lose as you, if anythin' happens to Amy.'

'Good enough. But I couldn't face Amy if anythin' happened to you.'

Luke laughed. 'You forget, I'm kinda good with my guns. I'm no greenhorn and would kinda relish a good shoot-out!'

'It's not a game, boy. No one waits to give a feller a sportin' chance. We backshoot 'em and they backshoot us if they can. You'll have to have eyes in your arse!'

'I can take it if you can.'

I poured more whiskey; it was the good stuff.

'Right! Just as long as I don't have to wet-nurse you!'

Luke acted a little affronted as he emptied his glass, put it down on the bar with a clatter and poured the rest of the bottle into it.

'Here's to us and to Amy, and to us watchin' each other's backs!'

I grinned and drank. I reckoned I couldn't have a better partner.

SEVEN

We left the little town of Santo Domingo early
the next mornin'. There was little traffic on the
windin' trail to the river-crossin'. It took two
days hard ridin' to get there and I watched
Luke closely for any sign of weakness. But
there was none. The boy sure was tough under
that youthful exterior.

The crossing of the Red River proved busy.
Several Conestoga wagons which floated when
on water, were lined up with a medley of lesser
vehicles which might not reach the other side
safely. It could be quite scary if some families
were swept away; I wasn't in the mood to waste
time in helping anyone in distress.

All I wanted was to get across that wide
expanse of water and keep ridin'.

There were cattle too, waitin' to cross. It seemed the Mexes liked to breed with Texan cattle. Somethin' to do with bone and meat structure.

We waited and drank a little at the lean-to bar which had sprung up beside the river. It was just as well we did so, for I heard all the latest gossip about who was runnin' things around these parts: who was wanted and who'd leaned against lead recently.

I say 'leaned against' in terms of who'd been gunned down, but I was more interested in who'd done the gunnin' than who'd got blasted. Some names I knew came up and I grinned at Luke, who was listenin' with open mouth like he was some greenhorn.

'Shut your mouth or you'll catch flies,' I said, and dug him in the ribs. He closed up like it was a trap.

'You know these men?' he asked quietly.

'Yeah, you might say that. Some of 'em anyway. We got ourselves an advantage, boy. We're not goin' in cold after Jordache. There's quite a few around here who remember what a swine he was.'

'You mean they'll throw in with us?' There was new respect in Luke's voice. He regarded me with awe and I liked it.

'Yeah, you might say that, and I've got somethin' with me that will persuade 'em if they're a bit unsure.'

'What's that then?'

I laughed and whispered in his ear, 'I kept one of those bars of gold. I thought it might do some persuadin' for us!'

Luke stared at me. I think he was shocked.

'But that's Government gold!' His voice rose a little.

'Keep your voice down, or someone might decide to tangle with us and then we'd have nothin' to dicker with!'

Luke gulped. He had a lot to learn, did that kid. He said no more and I considered the matter closed.

We splashed our way across that water and I nearly got carried away on account of a couple of hosses which panicked and sent their riders into deep water, crashing into us following behind. I cursed and saved myself from bein' flung overboard as well. I don't know what happened to the other riders, probably they were swept downstream. I couldn't have cared less.

We made up some time after we left that ford, passed a straggle of peasant-folk on the way and soon left them all behind.

When we rested up and let the horses browse, I cleaned Luke's wounds and fixed his bandage again. The wounds were healin' well – I'd feared the dirty water might have seeped into the bandages, but I needn't have worried. All seemed well.

After resting and eating we rode on. I was beginnin' to recognize the country again. It was time to keep an eye open for look-outs for we were comin' into dry desert country and a well-known area for owl-hoot hideouts.

I warned Luke to ride carefully and leave his rifle in the boot alongside his saddle. We also kept our hands in view. I wanted to give no wrong signals. We were ridin' through owl-hoot territory and wrong moves could mean a bullet in the back.

I was watchin' for a signal and I saw it on a far ridge. I glanced at Luke but he did not see it. He was ridin' easy and so I gave him no warnin' or else he might have acted nervous. That was one thing we shouldn't show, fear. We had to ride easy as if we were lords of that territory.

It paid off. Within an hour a squat barrel of a man with a sombrero that made him look like a mushroom, rode to meet us. He grinned and his teeth flashed under the finest set of moustachios I'd seen in an age.

'IIo there! State your business in these parts, *señors*. You're bein' watched from all sides, so be mighty respectful!'

I grinned at him.

'You're new around here or else you would recognize me,' I bluffed. 'I'm Two-Gun Starkey and I'm an old friend of Leon Ramirez, the scourge of Texas.'

The wolfish smile was wiped off that fat *hombre*'s face like magic.

'Two-gun Starkey? Are you joshin' me, señor, for if you are I'll skin you alive and feed you to the dogs!'

'I can prove it, pig-shit!' I drew my right gun with as smooth a draw as I'd ever done, and nicked his left ear.

There was the click of guns bein' cocked all around us and I swung round ready to blast anyone who moved. Luke was also quick on the draw and seven would-be shootists froze. It was a scary moment fraught with tension.

Then a stentorian voice from up on a ridge bellowed a warning.

'Hold everythin', *hombres*! I know this

pistolero man! Imbeciles! Do you all want to be filled full of holes?' A veritable giant of a man came leapin' down the rocks like some huge bear. He was grinnin' and holdin' out his hand and when he reached me I was enveloped in a bear hug. Then he held me away from him and looked me up and down.

'Two-gun Starkey! Where in hell have you been all these years? I thought you must be buried six feet under!'

'Leon Ramirez! You haven't changed a bit! Mebbe a bit more grizzled but you've still got the same gut!' I patted his firm round belly.

He lifted me high off the ground like I was a bag of feathers.

'Just the same old Leon, Starkey! What are you doin' in these parts, my old friend?'

It was time to be frank and blunt.

'I want your help, Leon. Jordache is in these parts and I'm after him.'

Leon Ramirez frowned and his eyes gleamed evilly

'If he thinks he can muscle in on my territory, he'll get a bullet in the back! I haven't forgotten or forgiven what he did all those years ago. It must be somethin' mighty serious to risk comin' back here.' He glanced at Luke and pointed with his thumb.

'Who's he?'

'My *segundo*. He ramrods my boys and is even faster with a gun than I was at his age.'

'And where are your boys now? Why do you need my help?'

'Because they're travellin' slow. They're bringin' in a king's ransom in gold!'

Leon Ramirez looked sceptical and Luke tried not to look amazed at my barefaced lyin'.

'You are what you Americanos call pullin' a fast one on your old friend?' he asked delicately, knowin' how fast fuses could be lit.

'What? Me pull a fast one over you, Leon, who's my friend? Here, take a look at this.' I leaned forward and opened my saddle-bag. He took a peek and drew a sharp breath as he glimpsed a hint of gold.

He stared hard at me. 'What you mean to do with all that gold?'

'I figured, seein' it was American gold, I'd offer it to a Mexican buyer who'd ask no questions. That bar of course, I'd give to the man who'd help me catch Jordache.'

Leon Ramirez laughed. 'I suppose your men are cachin' the bulk until the job's done, as a safeguard, eh?'

'Now you've got the picture, Leon. No offence. Just to be on the safe side. I don't want any of your men thinkin' to do you a favour by bushwhackin' Luke or me. I know you wouldn't let that happen ... would you?'

Leon laughed again, showin' his teeth and remindin' me that he looked like a hyena on the prowl. I knew damn well that there was no loyalty between thieves, just an on-the-surface pretence.

'You'd better come with us. You both look as if you could do with a good meal and a drink of tequila.' He strode away and we followed on horseback. His men followed on foot behind.

We passed over a natural bridge and into a hidden canyon which turned out to be a valley surrounded by high cliffs. In the valley bottom was a settlement of log cabins and corrals near a fast runnin' stream which fed a verdant pasture.

I envied the set-up. It was perfect for a hideout and the entrance to the canyon could be so easily defended. I looked at Leon Ramirez with admiration.

'You've got it made here, Leon. You're one hell of a lucky *hombre*!'

'And don't I know it!' he bragged, '*and* I've got

me three wives and ten *bambinos* and another on the way!'

That made me sit up. The son of a bitch wasn't that much younger than me and I'd been past it for years!

I thought of Amy, my one chick, and I ground my teeth. What I would do to that devil's spawn when I finally caught up with him! Ramirez's luck and the boast about his virility only fuelled my anger to boilin' point. I wouldn't rest until the job was done.

Ramirez's three wives waited on us and we fed well. One of them was old and the second was a prime piece about forty with a luscious body for a feller to get hold of, but it was the young one who took my eye. She wasn't much older than my Amy.

There were other women who came and looked us over and a bevy of children of all ages who belonged to Ramirez's followers. Luke got several covert invitations subtly conveyed by a liftin' of the eyebrows and a bit of tongue lickin' which showed those Mex women were all fire down below.

Luke ignored them all, which was a good thing. Chasin' one of them might have lit a powder fuse and I wanted all the help I could get to go after Jordache.

So we spent the night talkin' and makin' plans on how to locate Jordache. We drank more than a demijohn of tequila and it was good.

The upshot was that Ramirez was goin' to send out his scouts and infiltrate the rival gangs in the area and see if Jordache, accompanied by a woman, was claimin' asylum with someone.

So we lounged around, drinkin' and watchin' the women go about their business. I swear that all of 'em, even the old ones, loosened up their bodices for us to take a better look.

At least it gave Luke time to recuperate from his wounds and I know he'd not lost his sexual drive, for several times he groaned and walked with that peculiar gait of a feller sufferin' into the woods to relieve himself. This caused much raucous laughter from the women experienced in such things.

It was all that self-denial which made me realize that he truly loved Amy and would make her a good husband . . . if she was still alive and we got out of this mess.

Then Ramirez's scouts returned. I knew by their faces that Jordache had been located.

I rushed over to where the men were reportin' in to Ramirez, who was lookin' grave.

'They found the bastard, didn't they? Was there a girl with him?' I asked, waitin' with bated breath for the answer, for I'd not told Ramirez about Amy. The men turned and looked at me, a bit fish-eyed. I waited. Then Ramirez spat on the ground.

'You're not goin' to like this, Starkey,' he began.

'Jesus! For God's sake stop shilly-shallying Ramirez! Is the girl with him?'

'They don' know about no girl, but the bastard is holed up with Johnny Ratface up in the Sierras in that fortress of his ... you know, the one above Yaqui Pass on the Concho River.'

I barely heard him. I was thinkin' about Amy. Then it dawned on me and my heart stood still. Johnny Ratface was known to take prisoners and use them as slaves up in those mountains, lookin' for silver. If his prisoners happened to be women, then they too served a purpose. They were there to keep the workers happy. But would Jordache give Amy up so easily if he was usin' her?

I knew the answer to that. He would not, but mebbe he had no choice. Mebbe Jordache hadn't been so lucky with his friends.

'When do we start after him?' I grated harshly.

Ramirez blinked and looked uneasily at me.

'You *do* understand who we're up against? Johnny Ratface is one hell of a guy. He's not an *hombre* to mess with! He's half-Indian and knows some very nasty tricks and he's no lover of Americanos, I can assure you, *señor*.'

'Then how come Jordache could run to him?'

Ramirez shrugged eloquently. 'An old debt to be repaid? If there is a girl with him, mebbe he bargains with her. Johnny Ratface likes new faces.'

'Look, mister, if you and your men don't have the guts to go after this bogey-man, then we'll go alone. Mebbe we can do what you goddam fellers cain't do! Come on, Starkey, let's get ridin'!'

I spat at Ramirez's feet and turned to walk over to my hoss. I was conscious of Ramirez swellin' up with rage behind me. I wouldn't have bet on feelin' a slug might hit me between the shoulder-blades.

Instead, I heard his stentorian bellow.

'Hey, wait a minute, Starkey! You cain't let that young fool send you half-cocked against that madman up yonder!'

I turned and looked at him coolly.

'Luke's no fool and he's my pard. Where he

120

goes, I go. We'll do your dirty work for you, and rid you of that nest of scorpions!'

I sounded a damn sight more confident than I felt.

'How you do that, *señor*?'

'Show him that dynamite, Luke.' Luke obliged.

Ramirez's eyes bulged. 'Holy Mary,' he said and crossed himself. 'You've got the devil himself behind you! Mebbe he's workin' on our side at last!'

Then he turned to his men and gave them a lot of gabble in the local lingo. They nodded and looked with respect at Luke. Then Ramirez turned back to me.

'We ride with you in one hour, *señor*. We want to see that fortress blown to bits. We have many friends and relatives held up there and we want revenge on Johnny Ratface.'

'Then why are you standin' around wasting time?' I answered sharply. 'Get all the guns and ammo you can muster and we'll have us a little battle and us Americanos will show you what real fightin' is all about!'

It must have been the way I said it for Ramirez jumped to it and soon the whole camp was in an uproar. All the able-bodied men wanted to take part and when we rode out an hour later only boys and the old men were left in the camp to keep the cookfires burnin'.

Luke and Ramirez and me rode at the head of at least forty men bristlin' with guns and knives. I looked back at the long line of riders and I felt as I'd done in the old days.

There was an excitement singin' in my blood. I felt the energy flowin' through me. I was really alive again after years of hibernation. I glanced at Luke and smiled. I wondered what he was thinkin'.

He looked tense to me. I gave him a little wave and he acknowledged it. Everything would come right. We would kill that bastard Jordache. Luke would have Amy back and Ramirez would have the threat of Johnny Ratface removed for ever.

But of course it didn't quite turn out like that.

We drew rein at the ridge of a valley. We'd ridden all night and now the sun was comin' up over the far mountains, turnin' everythin' into a golden-red glow. We'd eaten as we rode and apart from stoppin' once to drink at a stream and water the horses, we were now ready for action.

Across the valley was the rearin' foothills of Mount Yaqui and as I shaded my eyes from the risin' sun I saw the crag near the top of that mountain permanently dusted with snow.

I nodded at Ramirez. 'That's it then, the famous fortress of Yaqui?'

Ramirez nodded back grimly. 'That's it. They say there's caves up there that go deep inside leadin' to tunnels that have been dug from early Maya times. They say that place can house a whole army if necessary. I should very much like to see you blow it apart, *señor* ... if you can!'

I heard the challenge in his voice. The bastards had only come to see us fail. I could understand that. It did seem a bit much. Two Americanos with a bunch of dynamite attemptin' to storm that stronghold. Well, we'd show the sons of bitches!

Ramirez had a pair of field-glasses slung around his neck. I gestured for them and I raked the mountain slowly, notin' the ledges and crags and the signs of buildin' and reinforcements. I also saw movement as if someone was on guard up there.

So Johnny Ratface wasn't too complacent about his eagles' nest. That meant there must be a weakness in the approach.

'Have any of your men been up there?' I asked casually.

Ramirez laughed. 'No, *señor*. Any man who goes up there never comes back!'

'Then how do your men know Jordache is up there?'

'They watched Johnny Ratface and some of his men ride by and Jordache was with them. A chance encounter, *señor*. They were lucky.'

'Hmm. So Jordache might not have been with friends. He might have been a prisoner?'

Ramirez lifted his shoulders.

'Either way, *señor*, he is up there.'

I glanced back at the waitin' men.

'We can't all go chargin' down there across that valley bottom. They would see us comin'.' Ramirez waited. I was clearly in charge. I ranged the valley bottom with the glasses and then came up with an idea.

Up there in that stronghold, water would be their priority and they would have to have a constant supply to cope with all those livin' up there. I concentrated on the Concho River windin' its way below. There would have to be a connection ...

Then I saw the makings of a plan. There would have to be a team of water carriers and if we could get near enough and overwhelm those teamsters, we could make our way upwards and into the fortress before the alarm was raised.

I also saw that if we rode along the ridge we could make our way through a forest of pines right down to the valley floor and then work our way along the river … It was ideal.

Luke laughed and Ramirez's eyes bulged when I outlined my plan. Ramirez looked at me with new respect.

'I see why you have been successful all these years, Starkey, ' he said with a certain amount of awe in his voice. 'You are a great leader and it has been a privilege to ride with you.'

Luke gave me a knowin' glance but kept his thoughts to himself. I would probably get ribbed about it later … if all went well.

So we backtracked a little so as to get beyond the skyline and picked our way down into the thick forest of trees. As the sun rose the shade was pleasant.

Down in the valley it was increasingly hot and several of the men dunked themselves in the shallows of the river before movin' on. Me and Luke didn't indulge. We knew what it was like to ride with a wet arse. It could cause sores and blisters.

Then, slowly and movin' like Indians, we made our way along the river bank, keepin' to the thick shrubbery. Then I called a halt and Luke and me started out to do some reconnoitring like I was used to doin' in the old days before a raid.

It brought it all back. The heightened senses, the poundin' of the heart, the alertness and readiness to jump any which way.

As we moved along we could see a wellworn track leadin' from the river. There seemed to be a natural ford at that part. The river flowed swiftly but shallow. There was much activity down there and several teams of horses and wagons were lined up. I'd guessed aright. The men were engrossed in fillin' large water tanks. As each tank was filled the driver and his mate moved off, each wagon being in charge of a man on horseback who carried a rifle at the ready. By that, I reckoned the driver and his mate were prisoners.

I also noted that the natural gradient was littered with all sizes of boulders and the trail had been handmade and cleared of debris.

I saw also that there were boulders big enough for men to hide behind as they clambered upwards. It would be quite easy for our little army to approach on foot.

There was one incident when Luke nearly fell over a man squattin' to do his business in the undergrowth. He opened his mouth to yell and Luke didn't hesitate, his knife took the man in the throat like a real professional. I was proud of him.

We found Ramirez nervously wanderin' up and down. He was a big feller and known as a good leader, but he wasn't up to the leadership I was accustomed to in the old days. Ramirez was a legend but in actual fact he was shit when it came to the real mayhem. I couldn't understand how he'd got his reputation. He was good at givin' orders but left it to his men to do the dirty work. Well, he was goin' to have to show a bit of grit now.

EIGHT

That assault up that slope was one of the hardest things I'd done in my life. Granted I was a bit old for that kind of caper, but to move forward and keep under cover took real Indian skill.

Ramirez and some of his boys took on the teamsters because some of those prisoners were already known to them. The guards, they soon disposed of them. Those boys were sure good with knives!

So it was easy for them. The same teamsters took on the haul up to the huge crag which had been turned into a fortress with the slow-movin' wagons containin' the huge metal tanks, and on the way, they gave Ramirez and his boys the low-down about what went on inside the huge complex which was in fact the head of an old silver mine.

The mountain was riddled with tunnels goin' down into the depths. The male prisoners diggin' for silver never saw daylight. The womenfolk lived in the first gallery underground and serviced the men and cooked for them.

Later, when I saw the dirty starved men and women totter out of those hell-holes with starin' eyes, blinded by the sun, I wanted to vomit.

Luke and I, who were leadin' the most agile climbers amongst Ramirez's crew, came across several caches of bones ... corpses flung down the mountain-side and picked clean by the buzzards, the bones bleachin' in the sun.

Those bones gave us the first indication of what was to come.

We were a grim, silent bunch when we neared the top. We had to wait in hidin' for the slow wagons to creak uphill. When the great wooden double doors opened we should storm the fortress and hopefully take the inmates by surprise.

It was a nerve-wracking time and the sun blazed down on us. There was also a crust of snow which never quite melted away in the sun's rays. It left behind a smooth hard ice that was slippery and one of Ramirez's men nearly wrecked our surprise by slippin' and crashin' down to the rocks below.

We left him there. There was no way he could have survived and any activity on our part would have put the whole operation at risk.

We were mighty glad to see the wagons. They came one behind the other, six huge tanks and I briefly saw that some of Ramirez's boys were bent double and coming up behind each wagon, which was good thinkin' on Ramirez's part. Mebbe that was how he had become leader – because he had imagination.

The twelve-foot-high doors creaked slowly open and the wagons moved forward. The first two entered the great natural plateau, then, taking advantage of the cover, we all charged in. Then all was screamin' confusion as guns blazed, knives flashed overhead seekin' targets and blood was spilled.

Durin' the first onslaught, men died who didn't even know they'd died. Soon there was a wall of bodies and still they came, shriekin' and yellin' obscenities, but now the early surprise was over and some of our boys fell. Johnny Ratface's men fought like demons.

But inch by inch we moved forward, beatin' them back until those still fightin' reached what was the main mine-shaft, where they took up a stance. It was then we got a salvo from further up the rocky fastness. Great slits had been hewn in the rock-face and now their guns blazed from inside what must have been a gallery.

I saw Ramirez, all blood and gore, his rifle useless and him wieldin' it like a club as the men went down before him. I lost contact with Luke early on and as the air grew thick with cordite and the stench of blood arose all around, I felt an exhilaration like that of a maddened animal.

I felt no fear. I was invincible. I tore a swath through the throng, for I had to find Jordache or Johnny Ratface and wreak some kind of revenge.

I felt a sting like a hornet and looked down and saw blood runnin' from my leg but I did not feel any real pain.

Then I saw Jordache and a man with him I surmised was Ratface himself. They were both at the head of the mine-shaft and they were usin' bullwhips on a shufflin' line of prisoners, makin' them move faster.

I saw their idea in a flash. They were goin' to use them as human shields. There were women amongst them, wild unkempt women with matted hair and hollow eyes. They and the male prisoners looked like a primitive species from an earlier time. They didn't look human.

I felt my guts heave. Was my Amy beginning to look like them?

Those pitiful half-humans kept pourin' out of that hole in the mountain like maggots out of a dunghill, and suddenly they were a barrier protectin' Jordache and Ratface and his head men.

Suddenly I went wild. I could stand it no longer. I had to do somethin' and I was ready to do something foolish, when Ramirez roared somethin' behind me in Spanish and goddammit, if the entire miserable crowd didn't fall flat on their faces!

I was astounded, then suddenly I saw Luke, a little behind Ramirez, raise his right arm in a wide arc and I knew what he was about to do.

I got down mighty quick and covered my eardrums and blast me to hell if I exaggerate, but that Luke sent that stick of dynamite high in the air. It landed on the top of the crag where Ratface and his boys were.

The whole world seemed to explode, rock splinterin' and flyin' like bullets and pieces of flesh splatterin' the surroundin' rock with what looked like red paint.

I was exhilarated until I thought of bein' robbed of killin' Jordache myself. Then there was Amy. Good merciful God, where was she?

That was when I let out such a roar, it sounded like a wounded bull even to my own ears. I hurtled my way through those prostate bodies, heedless of who I trod on. I just wanted to get to that ghastly still-smokin' hole and get myself below in those caves and tunnels and find my girl.

Behind me, dazed skeleton figures heaved themselves upright and stood like a flock of sheep waitin' for instructions. Then Luke was by my side and we fought our way to the centre of the mayhem.

We gazed down into a small crater showin' apertures that had been tunnels. We looked at each other and, without a word, scrambled down into what seemed to be hell. There were small fires ragin' where there had been wood supports to shore up weaknesses in the rock. There were bodies down there too, not all dead but many dyin'. There was the stench of cordite minglin' with human excreta as bowels evacuated with the shock of the blast.

I found Ramirez close behind us. There was an expression on his face I should never like to see again.

He was searchin' each body and lettin' each drop with a disgusted ugly look. He was lookin' for someone special. We were men with the same mission.

And while Ramirez searched he was mutterin' a string of curses enough to freeze the blood in a man's veins.

We were findin' more bodies alive now that we were movin' away from the centre of the blast; then Ramirez found Johnny Ratface half-laid and half-crouched against a juttin' rock. He was bleedin' freely and his face was badly damaged. He could not now be called Ratface, for he'd lost the two prominent front teeth and part of his mouth that had given him his name.

Ramirez swooped on him and dragged him up by his bloodied shirt; he shook him like a dog would shake a rat.

'You goddamn son of a bitch! What happened to my son! Answer me or I'll cut you up piece by piece until you do!'

The man's eyes bulged and his bleedin'

mouth worked but no words came forth. Ramirez took his knife and held it over one eye.

'Talk, scumbag, or else I'll gouge first one eye and then the other and then I'll start on your balls and on and on, until there's nothin' left of you!'

The answer was an attempt to spit at Ramirez. The knife twisted and blood spurted and the man screamed. I turned away. I had some huntin' of my own to do.

Luke was movin' ahead now and he'd found a firebrand still intact on a hook on the tunnel wall. We could now penetrate further into the cursed mountain-mine. I wondered if Jordache was still alive; there had been no sign of his body. Knowin' Jordache, I reckoned that when Ramirez yelled to the prisoners to drop he'd taken flight. The only way he could go was underground.

Guns at the ready, we moved along a main tunnel which was now not so strewn with loose boulders. There was a set of rails and then we came to small trucks, some containin' silver ore, others empty. Lines branched every which way as if all tunnels leadin' off came back to the main line.

It was becomin' a toss-up as to which tunnel we should explore; we settled to keep to the main line. There could be another outlet somewhere.

It was only luck that we reasoned right. We were roundin' a corner, the firebrand flarin' eerily in a sudden draught. Then a couple of bullets came whining past us, ricocheting from the walls and we ducked at the same time, Luke losin' his hat in the process.

And there was Jordache standin' far down the tunnel. In front of him he was holdin' Amy in a tight grip. I was never so relieved in my life to see her. It left me strangely weak.

'Hold it, fellers,' bellowed Jordache. 'One step nearer, and I'll blow her brains out!'

It was a stalemate, good and proper.

Luke's voice sounded cool.

'Let her go, Jordache, and we'll give you a head start. There's air comin' in from a shaft somewhere. We'll give you a break—'

Jordache laughed and his voice boomed hollowly along the passage.

'I'll take the break but the girl goes with me! You think I'm a fool? Your word means shit! You'd gun me down before she got clear!'

'Take her with you and we'll hunt you to hell! We'll never let up twenty-four hours a day. You want that?'

137

'I'll take my chances, buster. What about you, Starkey? You're mighty quiet!'

'I'm thinkin', Jordache. But I'm with Luke all the way. We'll hound you to hell!'

The answer was a rattle of bullets. I counted six spent all together and if he had a full clip in a second gun, he still had six to go....

Then, as we scrambled upright, he was draggin' Amy around a bend in the tunnel and I knew the bastard had already scouted a way out.

'Come on,' I shouted hoarsely to Luke. 'He's on the run!'

We followed at a stumblin' run and came to a fork in the passage. One passage was blowin' air, the other sloped steeply downhill; even a corpse would have known which path they'd taken.

We found this passage had a set of rails and I guessed it was an outlet for waste. I was right. At the top we came to several of the small trucks used to carry ore and tip it down the mountain.

Then we saw Jordache tryin' to free one of the trucks to send it careerin' down towards us. It was then that Amy began to fight and boy, did she make a good job of it!

She took him by surprise and I saw her grab up a rock as big as a man's fist and hit him on the side of the head. I could see a crimson stain spread over one cheek, even though he clawed for her. In the meantime, Luke put a spurt on and cleared the space between them before I could blink.

Then Amy was behind Luke and she came to me with arms outstretched, like a homing pigeon, while Luke tackled the dazed Jordache.

It was a mighty struggle and I stood with one arm around a saggin' Amy while in my other hand I held my gun at the ready for if Luke should need help.

But he didn't. It was some fight, for Jordache was at least three stones heavier than Luke and had a long reach and though he was hurt he was still strong and he fought like a wounded bear.

But youth had the advantage over age as it always has and I didn't need to use my gun. I saw Luke take him just as viciously as I would have done in my wild days, and he choked the life out of the big man.

I thought he would never leave go even after Jordache's thrashin' body lay still.

'Luke!' I called, 'it's all over!' Slowly he let the man go. He turned to us and shook his head several times as if forcin' himself back into normality. I knew how he was feelin'. I'd been in that state myself when I was more animal than human.

Then like an old man he came stiffly back to us and I saw the condition he was in. That fight had cost him much.

He was now a man who'd killed with his bare hands. The boy, Luke, was gone for ever.

Without a word, Amy turned from me, gathered her strength and silently slid into his arms. They clung together. Me forgotten.

NINE

I sat back in my chair rubbin' my leg and watchin' the little man in a dark store-bought suit and with a bowler hat sittin' on the back of his head, with tufts of fadin' ginger hair curlin' around it. My voice was hoarse with talkin' although I'd oiled my throat kinda often with the liquor in the demijohn at my feet.

He was a peculiar little man, sittin' hunched up and writin' notes in a little book. I'd never seen a man write so much, not even the clerk in court. He could talk too. He'd persuaded me to tell him all about our little caper when he'd read about Luke and me discoverin' a cache of stolen bullion and returnin' it to a grateful government who, incidentally, had paid us what

I considered to be a poor reward for what we did, seein' as to the danger and discomfort to us.

We had been in all the newspapers back East and were kinda famous and then this little feller had come off the train at Abilene and found his way to us. He told us of his long trail lookin' for us from back East and so I couldn't refuse to tell him about what happened. But it was his promise of payment for same rather than his silver tongue that persuaded me.

Mind you, no one knew the reluctance I had about returnin' that gold to an ungrateful government. It was the only one time Luke and me had a huge bust-up and he won.

For all the potential the boy had for becomin' a successful outlaw, havin' the speed and know-how about shootin' and the courage to get in there and use his fists, he was still a sheriff at heart and a law-abidin' feller. That gold had to go back where it came from.

It wasn't that I backed down easy. But he threatened to tell Amy all about my past and I wasn't havin' that. The young son of a bitch had me over a barrel and if I wanted to sit his kids on my knee I should have to set myself down and become respectable once again, which was mighty hard after that bit of excitement and I'd found I was still quite capable of the rough stuff after all.

Still, I did have trouble with my leg and it was kinda nice to be looked after. I could spend my time on the ranch, for Luke and Amy had taken over the bar I ran and it was now famous because of the gold business. Luke had even renamed it from Starkey's Bar to The Bullion Bonanza and folk came in from far and wide to gawp at it and then have a drink inside so they could boast to their buddies back home.

So now I looked at this scribblin' little feller. He'd already told me some hair-raisin' tales about how he got his plots for his books. For this was Edward Z C Judson, the feller known as Ned Buntline in the publishing business. I thought it strange for a feller like him to have an alias. I usually associated criminals with aliases.

Oh, he might not look it, but he was a live wire all right, and wealthy enough through these books he wrote to retire and enjoy life.

Mind you he did that an' all. Last night we'd both been on a bender an' he told me about his many marriages and the trouble they'd caused him. He also told me about his friendship with

Wyatt Earp and Bill Cody and a whole string of names I've forgot.

I'm not sure whether I believed half the things he told me in his cups, but it was fascinatin' listenin' to him.

So there I was, watchin' him scribble with a sure fist. I wished I could write so fast. My efforts usually brought my tongue out in my effort to write proper and I would finish up in a sweat.

Now I was suddenly havin' second thoughts of what I'd told him. Mebbe I'd gone into too much detail. I leaned forward in my chair.

'You're sure now you'll change names. You said all this was confidential and that all you want is a plot?'

He nodded, still writin' vigorously.

'Yeah … yeah, no sweat, mister,' he muttered. 'Where did you say the gold was buried?'

'I didn't say,' I answered flatly.

'Are you gonna tell me?'

'No! You have to use your own imagination for a change,' I said snappily. He was payin' me one thousand dollars for this account of our doin's and it had to remain a secret from Luke who was well out of it, lookin' after our bar.

I was feelin' uneasy. What if, when the story

144

came out, Luke got wind of it and it was too near real life? What would his reactions be?

I could offer him half the cash, mebbe that would satisfy him. Then of course he might never know. He was no reader of books. He was a man of action.

But if he *did* find out, then how could I explain not splittin' the cash?

Oh, hell, mebbe I should have kept my mouth shut and not been tempted to tell all.

Judson's or, should I say, Buntline's question about the location of the gold had reminded me of what had happened when it was dug up.

That had been a scary episode in itself and I sure wasn't havin' this little squirt knowin' about it.

Luke had his little map safe and when we rode out with Amy from that hellish place, we made straight for the gold. Luke and me had argued about this. I wanted to leave it hidden until we'd got Amy home safely. The girl was mighty distressed and didn't look like my pretty little girl any more. She was haggard and hollow-eyed and I knew she'd been through a lot by the way she eyed Luke at night, for after that one joyous hug when we freed her, she kept well away from him and I knew why.

That son of a bitch, Jordache had used her and used her rough.

She was now frightened of men, even of me. I wanted to kill that bastard all over again even though he was dead. He'd got off too lightly. I hoped he would burn twice over in Hell.

It had been a nightmare ride afterwards. It's strange how the smell of gold attracts mayhem. There's something about it that can't be hidden. We had more owlhoots, drifters and conmen around us on that journey than a honeypot attracts wasps.

We left a trail of death and destruction behind us and Luke sure got his bellyful of potshottin' and backshootin'; enough to last him all his life.

But somehow, we got that gold back East and when Amy and I got back to our ranch, Luke reckoned he could ride right on to Washington with that gold bullion as bold as brass.

I reckoned he would lose it along the way, but he was adamant that he would try. Now that he had no Amy to hold him back and he figured to give her time to adjust, for her attitude to him hurt him very much, he did the impossible.

Afterwards, he told me he travelled at night, laid up durin' the day and avoided towns and such, and he used the backtrails. I reckoned he was one smart boy.

Then of course came all the hoo-ha when he rode into Washington to the Treasury and calm as you please reported the safe return of the gold bars.

I would have liked to see those pen-pushers' faces when they saw what those chests held. Mind you, they huffed and puffed a bit when they checked back and found there were some bars missin'. Bastards like them are never grateful. Of course Luke knew about me nickin' the bars in the first place when I told him about my past. I'd also kept that one bar when we came back and I still had it and I was gonna give it to my first grandchild.

He told a likely story about about the missin' gold bein' lost at the time of the raid, and who could prove otherwise after thirty years?

So there it was, the biggest story for years and I suppose a lot of folk who read about it thought Luke was a fool. He should have kept it. That alone made him a kind of saint, someone different from the common folk.

Anyway, Luke got to meet the President himself and got a picture to prove it of him and the great man shakin' hands. He was right proud of that. So much so, he's sometimes hard to live with.

Buntline looked at me.

'Anything else you can tell me?'

I felt as if the feller was suckin' me dry.

'What more do you want? Surely that's enough?'

'What about your daughter? What were her reactions? After all she went through a bad time.'

'Yes,' I said warily. 'She did suffer.'

'Could I talk to her?' He said it kinda cold. My legs worked and I was for gettin' up and punchin' him, but I controlled myself.

'I'm sorry. She's very shy and retirin', and she's what you might call in an interestin' condition.'

He cocked a sly eye at me.

'Oh,' he said and winked, 'it's like that, is it? It's not the outcome of what happened with Jordache? I mean to say, you were pretty blunt about what happened to her!'

I did punch him then and he fell off his chair and his book and pencil flew down along the veranda.

He scrambled to his feet, fingerin' his jaw, then gathered up his things.

'You didn't have to do that, Mr Starkey, sir. It's what a mighty lot of folk would think!'

'Well,' I growled, 'this child is Luke's and there's no mistake if you can reckon on dates! After all, all what I told you happened more than two years ago, so use your head!'

'It would add a kind of pathos to the tale for the female readers if the heroine was done wrong,' he muttered as he adjusted his steel-rimmed spectacles which I wasn't sure whether he needed or not as they were on and off his nose so many times.

I perked my ears up.

'You get womenfolk readin' those yarns of yours?' I asked with astonishment. 'I thought women had better things to do, like housework and rearin' kids than to sit idle, readin'.'

'Of course, Mr Starkey and that's why I want to know about your daughter's reactions! I know all about the kidnapping and the – er – treatment Jordache made her suffer but did she talk about the time she was held in that infamous mine? What about her reactions to the prisoners and their sufferin'? She must have had some thoughts on the subject.'

I stared at him. He didn't see any of us as real people. We were just characters to put in his books.

I thought back to Amy and how she'd been when we started out on that trek back home. She'd been withdrawn, out of this world, had moved automatically and cried a lot when she should have been asleep. And she wouldn't let Luke or me comfort her. It had been a bad time and never once had she talked about her time in the mine. It was somethin' we never probed. We wanted her to put it all out of her mind, and now this little scumhound from back East expected to winkle out every emotion and hurt she'd ever experienced.

I nearly snatched his precious book and told him to get to hell off my land. Then I remembered the one thousand dollars. I wanted it as a gift for my grandchild.

'Look, mister, Amy never talked about those unfortunate people held in Johnny Ratface's silver mine. If you want to know about them, get down into Mexico and talk to some of the survivors. They'll give you enough stuff for several yarns. Go find Ramirez who lost his son to Johnny Ratface and found other relatives he'd thought had gone for ever, in that hellhole. You don't have to suck my Amy dry to find out what you want!'

'Hmm, mebbe I'll just do that. These tales of

blood and guts go down well back East. I kind of keep the West alive for those who won't go West and find out for themselves.'

'You make it sound romantic and it's not.'

'Sure, you know that and I know that but my readers don't! It's folk like you who make me rich. You know that, Mr Starkey?' He was grinnin' at me now. I didn't like it. He was bein' condescendin' as if we all had more brawn than brain.

'I think it's time you were on your way, Mr Buntline, or whatever you call yourself.' I think he sensed a certain warnin' in my voice.

'Just another few questions, Mr Starkey, if you don't mind.'

'I do mind,' I said cautiously. 'You can ask but I don't promise to answer them.'

'All this you've told me, it *is* true, isn't it?'

'Yes,' I said carefully, 'it's all true, but you've got to alter all names and locations or I'll sue you in the courts!'

'I guarantee you'll not know yourself, Mr Starkey, when I finish writing what I'm going to write. But what I want to know is, what you told me about your earlier life, is that true too?'

'Ah, so that's it, isn't it? That's what you really want to know! Now why is it important that it should be true or not?'

He shrugged.

'Just curiosity on my part. It makes it all so much better if I know that your reactions were genuine and how a retired old owlhoot would actually react in those circumstances. After all, you might have had as much imagination as I have, sir.'

'Well, I assure you, it's all true and you can take my word for it that I should do the same again if necessary. Once an outlaw, always an outlaw!'

'Could I quote you on that? I mean just as a character in my story?'

I gazed at him steadily. I was really havin' second thoughts about all this. Mebbe I shouldn't have swallowed so much of that rot-gut liquor.

'Look, Mr Buntline, or whatever your name is, mebbe we should call this all off. I don't like the idea of you makin' so much about the outlaw business. Mebbe my imagination's as good as yours and I put in all that just to pep things up!'

He winked, goddamn him! and went on scribblin'.

'Mr Starkey, I got me a plot for a new tale and

no way will you and yours be embarrassed by same. So you might as well keep the cash like a sensible feller. You don't have to read the book and nobody in these parts need know about it. Right? Does that ease your mind?'

'I just don't want Amy to know ...' I muttered between my teeth.

'I understand that, Mr Starkey. All fathers want to stand tall with their offspring. You'll have no worry on that score.'

'Well, you'd better remember it, mister, for as I said, once an outlaw, always an outlaw!'

'Are you threatening me, Mr Starkey?'

'You might say that, sir!'

He looked distinctly uncomfortable – like a man ready to shit his pants.

'I think it's time I was taking my leave, Mr Starkey, sir. The buggy's waiting and I've a train to catch.'

I rose creakily from my chair and straightened up, conscious of my bowed shoulders.

'Well, it's been a pleasure to talk, Mr Buntline ...'

'Mr Judson, please. Mr Edward Z C Judson.'

'Well, whatever your name is, it's been a pleasure I don't get often. Just remember, sir, old outlaws never change!'

I watched him move mighty fast and climb into the buggy. I knew the driver, old Ned, and gave him a wave and they were off, travellin' at a rare clip down my dirt road.

I sensed a movement behind me and there was Amy watching. Fleetingly I wondered how much she'd overheard but by her face she hadn't heard much, if anythin'.

She came and stood beside me.

'What a strange little man, Pa. Are all men like him from back East?'

I laughed and shook my head.

'He's a one and only, is that one. You can forget him, love.'

TEN

She sat down beside me rather heavily as she was so near her time. She had blossomed again in these last six months and now it was hard to realize that for many months Luke and I had despaired that she would ever be our Amy once again.

It had taken months of patience on Luke's part to bring life back into those haunted eyes. There was no emotion or laughter there and to think of it now still brought a shudder ripplin' up and down my spine.

There were times when all she would do was roam the land so that she was free to come and go as she liked. Luke followed at a distance to watch over her and see that she did no harm to herself. It was an unspoken dread we shared that she might take her own life.

Durin' that time it was I who ran the bar and coped with rubbernecks who came on account of the publicity of what Luke had done. I only visited the ranch when time allowed. Luke took over the managin' of the ranch and did it so well that he gave up his job as sheriff.

But time is the great healer and gradually Amy began to trust us again. Even now, though, she is wary about meetin' strangers and that was why she would not meet Judson.

One mornin' I heard her laugh for the first time in months. It burst from her like the chirrupin' of a songbird. I glanced out of the window and saw her and Luke leadin' in two horses and realized that they had been ridin' together. The sound of her laughter lifted my heart. I wanted to hug and kiss her but I controlled the urge. It might have sent her back into that place we could not enter.

From then on, she began to eat and put on the weight she'd lost and she began to take pride in herself, in her body and her clothes, both of which had been sadly neglected.

The rest I left to Mother Nature and she didn't let me down.

Amy responded again to Luke and the love

she'd known before finally surfaced and I could see that the situation between them meant quick action. I got them both to church and standin' before the preacher and takin' their vows before they knew what hit them.

Now, there was to be a grandchild soon, the first of many, I hoped. It would be good to sit back and relax and let the babies crawl all over me and some day, mebbe tell them tales of long ago, well watered down of course.

Now we sat, watchin' the buggy disappear into the distance. She spoke first.

'I'm glad he's gone, Pa. I like this place with no strangers around.'

'I know, love. It won't happen again.'

She turned to me, tears glistening in her blue eyes.

'I never really told you how much I love you, Pa. You did a brave thing goin' after Luke when he set out to look for me. I never thought of you as a fighting man, Pa. You've always been just Pa to me, someone quiet and reliable who looked after me and picked me up when I fell down. Luke told me how brave you were and what you both went through to find me. Thanks, Pa.' She put her hand in mine and leant over and kissed my cheek.

I was hornswoggled. We weren't much on the kissin', never had been when she was knee-high to a grasshopper. Mebbe it was because of Luke teachin' her or somethin'.

I patted her clumsily on the shoulder and my arm stayed around her, somethin' she wouldn't have allowed me to do a few months earlier.

'There ... there ... I only did what was the right thing,' I mumbled, wonderin' what the hell Luke had told her.

She sighed and cuddled in a bit under my arm.

'Pa, d'you think Luke's changed a bit lately?'

'Changed? In what way?'

'Well, kind of aggressive. He's not the Luke I remembered.'

'The boy's all grown up. He's a man now,' I answered gruffly. 'Y'know, he went through hell and back when you were with ...' I hesitated. I hated speakin' that rat's name.

Her hand pressed mine. She didn't need any name.

'I know, but it's more than that. There's a dark streak in him, Pa, that wasn't there before.'

'Honey, there's dark side to all men and good men control that dark side. Luke's a good man and he'll never let you down.'

She turned her expressive blue eyes on me.

'But you've never had a dark side, Pa. You've always been open and honest and had no secrets. Why can't he be like you?'

I reached for the demijohn and took another gulp of raw liquor to give me time, for I couldn't have met her eyes. I felt like a goddamn snake in the grass. Jesus! If she only knew!

I shuddered inwardly. I cursed my wayward youth.

I looked into the far distance, wonderin' how to answer her. Then it came to me that if I hadn't been what I was, then Amy might not be sittin' safely beside me today. I grinned at her.

'Don't worry. Luke will be just like me some-day!'